D1364342

Once
A Stranger

NEIL ADDINGTON is the first of the real and human characters who people *Once a Stranger*. Anxious to finish his latest novel in the shortest possible time, he rents a cottage in the quiet village of Westington, intending to cut himself off from every human contact.

But in the subtle development of Margaret Yorke's tale, he finds that he cannot remain withdrawn from the village and, as life in the small community has its effect upon him, his outlook changes.

It is Anna Harris whose life is altered immeasurably by Neil's coming. Her marriage to Tom Cartwright has been postponed and, restless and unhappy, she meets Neil when both are at a disadvantage; later, she begins to help him prepare his manuscript, and finds that she has embarked also upon a journey to greater knowledge of herself.

MARGARET YORKE

Once A Stranger

This edition published in Great Britain 1988 by
SEVERN HOUSE PUBLISHERS LTD of
40–42 William IV Street, London WC2N 4DF.
First published 1962 by Hurst & Blackett Limited.

British Library Cataloguing in Publication Data
Yorke, Margaret
Once a stranger.
I. Title
823'.914 [F]
ISBN 0–7278–1675–8

Printed and bound in Great Britain

I

Neil

THE cottage lay round a bend near the top of the hill where, after its winding journey from the village half a mile below, the lane ended abruptly in a stout fence. Lilacs, their boughs heavy with white and purple blossom, clustered round the long, low building, hiding its windows from any curious passer-by; but, as the agent had maintained when I signed the lease, it was unlikely that anyone except a casual walker would penetrate this remoteness. Seclusion seemed ensured.

The taxi driver, a younger man than I, brought in my bags and typewriter, and I paid him for the journey from Chawton station. He climbed back into his car, turned quickly in the narrow space of the lane, sending flint chippings flying with the friction of his tyres, and filling the mild evening air with the smell of petrol fumes. As he left, I closed the wicket gate behind me and walked back up the short path to the front door. It was painted pale blue, a strident modern touch in contrast with the old beams and mellow bricks. With its soft-coloured tiled roof it was, as the agent had declared, 'a Tudor gem'; but succeeding generations had sharpened its facets in a manner that added to its comfort and embellishment without in any way detracting from its charm. No wonder the rent was high, I thought. London, the noise, the

7

shock, the horror of all that had been preying on me for the last month, seemed no longer to exist.

The front door opened straight into the living-room of the cottage. It was long and narrow, with a wide fireplace at one end and small leaded windows along both sides. The furniture was angular and modern, but unlike the colour of the front door it was somehow not incongruous and the impression the room gave was immediately one of restfulness and comfort. A settee upholstered in dark blue rep stood at right-angles to the hearth, and two deep chairs, one red and one grey, completed the conventional semi-circle. There were several cushions, patterned in stripes, and the plain cream carpet was, I saw in surprise, new. A few good sporting prints hung on the walls; and at the end of the room farthest from the fireplace there was a small oak dining-table, sturdy enough for the type-writer, with four wheel-back chairs pushed close to it. I soon discovered that the rest of the cottage was in keeping with this room, though the bedroom furniture looked as though it had been gathered together in a more hap-hazard fashion. The kitchen was brightly painted in pale yellow: I grimaced at the choice; on bad days this colour scheme would not be uplifting.

The thought brought me back to facts and I remembered. Grimly, I opened one of my suitcases and took out the brandy bottle that I had opened in the train. After a short search I found a tumbler and poured a generous amount into it; my hand shook and I spilled some of the stuff as I slopped it out of the bottle. I felt better after I had swallowed it, and I set about sorting out my luggage. Stupidly, I had not thought of asking the taxi driver to carry the heavy suitcases upstairs, and by the time I had completed the task I was out of breath and gasping. I chose the smaller of the two bedrooms, which opened out of one another in the customary way of such old dwellings, because it was at the back of the cottage away from the lane. The bed, a high, old-fashioned one, was comfortable, and the furniture was painted white, like a child's, but the room was pleasant. I speculated briefly about my landlord, a farmer who owned the neighbouring land. It seemed curious that he should possess such a property; there must be very little demand to rent a place of this sort in a district remote from any industrial or commercial centre. Possibly there was a military installation nearby and succeeding service families came and went with the years. If so, they had left no trace of wear and tear behind them. Perhaps the landlord kept a stern, supervising eye upon his tenants: he had better not attempt that with me. My only desire was to be left completely alone to finish my work away from problems and conflicts. For this reason I had refused the agent's offer to engage a village woman to undertake the housekeeping and cleaning.

Now, though, I regretted this decision as I searched for bed-linen and towels. It was too difficult after the journey, and I was much too tired; swearing, I abandoned the task of making up my bed and stumbled down the stairs again to find the brandy.

It was morning when the shrill twittering of birds in the bushes round the cottage came into my consciousness. At first I could not remember where I was: there was the usual pounding in my head, my tongue felt thick and my mouth was full of the sour taste of morning. The strangeness of hearing no traffic bewildered me; for a moment, with near hysteria, I thought that I was back again in the hospital. Soon, Nurse Martin's sharp heels would come clicking along on the lino and I would see her round, important face bending over me. But then I remembered: that was all over now.

I sat up. It was no surprise to find that I had never gone to bed; I was sprawled on the elegant dark-blue settee with my shoes on. I winced as the movement made my head reel. My vision was blurred and my eyes ached. I lowered my feet to the floor, and there was a small sound as they landed on the glass tumbler that had lain on its side on the new cream carpet all night. First casualty, I thought wryly. No doubt there would be others, but someone else could worry about that; at least there was no longer any need to worry about money, thanks first to Fenella, and thanks also to *The Breakers* which had run into ten impressions, and earned me thousands when it had been made into a film – thousands for the rights alone, and more for my supervision of the script, though by the time it had been cut and edited precious little of the script was in fact my work.

I stood up, grinding the rest of the glass into fragments as I did so, and lumbered out into the kitchen.

After a time I felt better: the open back door admitted a stream of bright sunlight, and still the birds sang. It was years since I had heard such a sound, one that had never been a familiar part of my life, for cities were where I belonged. I groped about for the brandy bottle; a hair of the dog would pull me round. Then Nurse Martin's face swam into my mind again and I heard her hearty morning voice:

'A nice cup of tea, Mr Addington, just to set you up for the day. Now don't let it get cold.'

Since everything was irrevocably different now, my daily habit might change too. I searched about for a kettle. Tea, dark and sugarless; a panacea, but not for me.

I found the kettle, but of course there was no tea, nor any milk. I had run away from my problems so hastily that I had never thought about such mundane things. I cursed. No doubt there was a village store of some kind in Westington where I would be able to buy food of a sort. Later I would arrange with a shop in Chawton to deliver supplies at regular intervals. I would draw up a standing order.

How astonished Fenella would be if she could see me now, marooned by choice in the remotest country village in the Home Counties, planning my purchasing like any housewife, and hiding from my fellows like a fugitive from the law. Ah, well, retribution would follow me in time, just as in the end justice would catch the wrong-doer, I supposed. Meanwhile, there was another bottle of brandy and I opened it.

Later, I went upstairs. My cases were in the disorder that I had abandoned the night before, open, with half their contents strewn across the room and shoes in a huddle on the floor. As I bent to pick them up my head swam, and groaning, I lay down on the bed. I closed my eyes, but the noise of the birds outside, and the queasiness of my own stomach stopped me from going into another sleep, so that soon I got up again and walked across to the window, where I stood looking out at two starlings quarrelling on the grass below.

Presently, a distant movement distracted my attention

from the birds' antics, and I looked away from them down the hill. To the south of the cottage there was a small garden which sloped away to a stile leading into a field. This was the same field that curved round to meet the lane by the fence I had seen the evening before. There were cows grazing in the field, short sturdy black ones; I didn't know what sort and I didn't care. I realized that one of them had made the movement I had noticed, and then I saw the cause of their disturbance: a small white dog. It ran to and fro among them, sniffing at the ground. The cattle looked at it suspiciously, heads lowered, and a few of them lumbered away from it; but one, more bold, advanced towards it curiously. I heard a faint whistle, and then a voice calling. Looking on down the hill I saw the solitary figure of a woman, walking. She must be an early riser; I hoped she did not make a habit of coming this way daily at such an hour, though I was unlikely often to awake so soon myself.

She drew nearer, walking among the cows with calm familiarity that I could envy, the dog running on in front. I saw then that there was a faint, worn track of flattened grass leading from the stile across the field along the way that she was coming, and I realized that someone must have often walked here; it was probably a shorter route to the village than the twisting lane provided. I watched as the woman approached. She reached the stile and put her hand on it to climb over, looking up as she did so. I ducked back quickly out of sight, and when I looked again she had crossed it and was coming through the garden, slowly, bending to pull something from one of the flowerbeds and stopping to look back at a little cluster of faded daffodils now withered in the grass. She walked on up to the house and out of sight; I realized she had entered by the back door.

Before I had time to do more than wonder at such an extraordinary occurrence the dog came scrabbling into my bedroom, snuffed round my feet and vanished. I heard it scuttling down the stairs, and then it began to bark; a shrill yapping filled the house: hideous.

I began to follow the dog down the stairs, but any noise my footsteps made on the polished treads was drowned by its din. The stairs descended into a corner of the living-room at the side nearest to where the table stood, and I paused on the lowest step. Across the room, over by the fireplace, the woman crouched on hands and knees by the sticky mess of the broken brandy glass. Her back was towards me, but I could see that she was picking up the fragments. Meanwhile the dog danced round her, still yapping. She said something to it, crossly, and stood up. She was short, sturdily built, with brown hair arranged in no particular style, and she was dressed in a worn tweed skirt and shabby leather jacket. The dog pranced about; foolish creature, it had not observed that I, the cause of all its commotion, had come into the room. It cavorted round and knocked into the brandy bottle that I had left on the floor; there was still a trickle left in it, and it ran out on to the carpet. The woman muttered something angrily, and with her foot she thrust the dog roughly out of the way before stooping again to retrieve the bottle. There was abrupt silence as the barks ceased; the dog did not whine, it merely stared at her with an expression of almost human incomprehension on its face. I was startled by the sudden crude, almost vicious action.

'That wasn't very pretty,' I said.

She swung round at once, leaping up quickly, her hands full of broken glass. My first impression was that she was nearly crying. She sniffed and said in a loud, defiant voice: 'This is your filthy mess, I suppose.'

I came on down the stairs and across the room towards her. She was plain, and not young; in her thirties, I judged. Her brown eyes, with heavy lines round them, glared at me. She was all brown, her hair, her clothes, even her skin was tanned.

'Who are you? What are you doing here?' she demanded.

I saw that the fright my sudden appearance had given her was yielding now to anger, and I realized that the tears which threatened her were of rage. She seemed to remember suddenly that both her hands were full, and without waiting for my reply she hurried out of the room, exclaiming something under her breath, returning almost immediately without the glass and carrying a cloth. Pushing past me she began at once to rub furiously at the spilt brandy.

'I think it is I who should ask who you are, since I am the tenant of this cottage,' I told her bent profile. 'You are the intruder, not I.' I was pleased with the flowery, pompous remark and waited to see how she would reply.

She went on rubbing, but more slowly; then she stood up and looked at me. The anger had left her face; she seemed bewildered.

'But you were coming tomorrow. No one should have been here. The cottage should have been empty,' she cried accusingly. There was a note of childish protest in her voice.

'I came last night. The agent had given me the key and my lease runs from the first of the month. There was no reason for me to delay,' I said, still waiting for her to explain herself.

'Oh,' she said. 'I see.' She was trying to adjust herself to accept this lawful justification of my presence. Now that her anger had departed she appeared forlorn and uncertain. 'I'll just finish clearing this up,' she mumbled, hurrying away once more. This time she returned with a dustpan, and in a few minutes, apart from a damp patch on the carpet, there was no trace of the baptism it had received. Meanwhile the dog had lost all interest in what was happening and had vanished.

'I'm sorry I was so rude,' said my visitor at last. 'I suppose you had an accident, but this is a new carpet.'

She was in command of herself now, but her fingers, twisting nervously round the dustpan, which she held shield-like before her, betrayed her nervousness. It occurred to me that I might present a fearsome spectacle: I was unshaven, and I knew that my eyes must be red-rimmed and yellow, while my face was doubtless grey.

'I can see it's new,' I said. 'So is most of the furniture.'

'I hope you like it,' she said vaguely, looking round. 'We – it's partly mine. I'm Anna Harris. Tom Cartwright, who owns the cottage, is my fiancé. I often come – came here.'

'I see.' I was surprised. The oddly formal way in which she explained her connexion with my landlord struck me as quaint; she was hardly one's idea of an engaged girl, and I imagined him to be a rugged, bucolic bull of a man, no longer young, perhaps a widower. Highly suitable, I decided, grinning to myself as I observed that her large, capable-looking hands were slightly red. She was certainly a strong, rustic type herself, though her speech made it clear that she was not of the village.

'I'll go now. I'm sorry. I wouldn't have come if I'd known you'd arrived,' she said. 'You don't want to see anyone, I know.' She turned away. 'I only came to say good-bye,' she said.

'Good-bye?' I was curious, as a writer must always be, about even the most humdrum circumstance. It ran through my mind that she had quarrelled with her farmer and the match was off; she wore no ring; and hence, presumably, the fact that the cottage was let.

'Oh – I suppose it sounds silly,' she said. 'Tom and I were going to live here – we were getting married next week. We'd spent the winter painting, and getting furniture and things – this carpet, and so on.'

'What happened?' Perhaps she had decided that she would be safer with her dog.

'Oh, Tom's father died suddenly – in a motor accident it was – six weeks ago, and his mother's been very ill ever since. She had a heart attack. Tom can't leave her.'

'So you've postponed the nuptials?'

She shrank from the mockery in my voice; she noticed it, then.

'Just for a while,' she said flatly. 'I'm sorry – you don't want to hear all this.'

'Oh, but I do. I'm passionately interested,' I told her. 'Why did you decide to let the cottage? Don't you want it now?'

'Yes, but we don't know when we'll be able to get married. It all depends on Mrs Cartwright. Tom will have to stay at Combe – that's the farmhouse – now. If Mrs Cartwright ever recovers she'll come up here, but goodness knows when that will be. So when Mr Foster, the agent in Chawton, said there was someone wanting to rent an isolated cottage we decided to let it. As Tom said, it isn't good for a place to be empty, and we could use the money for more furniture. It's sense, really.'

'It is, indeed,' I agreed. 'And so you came up here on a romantic farewell pilgrimage and found a broken glass desecrating your carpet,' I said. 'It doesn't sound as if you've got an ideal tenant, does it?'

She stared at me doubtfully; hurt, her eyes looked larger.

'Well, I'm not,' I told her. 'I'm bad-tempered; I can't sleep; I'm rude and lazy, ill-mannered, and I drink like a fish. There!' I grinned at her maliciously. 'But my cheques don't bounce and I'll pay adequate compensation for the damage I'm certain to cause.'

'I don't expect it will be as bad as you make out,' she said uncertainly.

'You'll see for yourself,' I told her. 'In fact, you'd better come up here sometimes and have a look at your precious carpet – keep the score of the stains. Only leave that damned dog behind, I can't stand yapping. Come to that, I don't think you've shown up yourself in too good a light today, have you?'

She blushed and hung her head.

'I lost my temper,' she confessed. 'Toby irritates me.'

'Well, if you're not afraid of me, come and see the

scene of your shame,' I said. 'But don't say you haven't been warned.'

So this was how I began my sojourn in isolation, unable to resist provoking a vulnerable and unskilled victim.

2

Anna

I'VE been sleeping so badly lately. It's making me jumpy and cross, like that neurotic woman in the strip advertisements. What Tom sees in me I can't think. I don't suppose he does see much; there isn't anything very romantic about either of us, and it's no good me trying to weave a dramatic situation out of it, or a romance around Neil and me.

Neil. It's a funny name, I've never known a Neil before. But then I don't know this one really; I wonder if anyone does? You never know what he's thinking. What a way to meet! I'd woken up very early that morning, and I just couldn't go to sleep again. I'd been worrying about the cottage, hating the idea of anyone else using our things. I've always loved that cottage; I'm not sure I don't love it more than Tom, though that's an awful thing to think. Everyone says I've no imagination, but I like to wonder about the people who must have lived there for hundreds of years past, some that we know about, and others that we don't. People have been born there and died there, been miserable sometimes, but been happy there too. Tom and I would have been happy there. I suppose we will be at Combe, it shouldn't make any difference; that's a friendly, nice house, but I dread the thought of Mrs Cartwright being there all the time, for years and years, lying in bed getting smaller and frailer and less like herself, shrinking in front of us, having to be thought about all the time. She'll never recover enough to go to the cottage, even with a nurse. I'm sure Tom knows that really, he just goes on deceiving himself that she's getting stronger, when all the time she seems to be going farther away. I was fond of her, but now I'm afraid when I go to see her, she's so different. I can't think of anything to talk about, I'm sure she doesn't really want to be bothered with me. Poor Tom, it's dreadful for him, first his father and now this. The least I can do is to try and not bother him and add to his worries. He's right to let the cottage; it was luck that the house agent knew about it and had a tenant for it. I must pull myself together and stop acting like a sentimental schoolgirl over it. But the trouble is, I am still a schoolgirl inside. Nothing has ever made me anything else; things don't happen to people like me.

But I was remembering the morning when I met Neil. That, anyway, I'll never forget. When I'd given up the idea of going back to sleep I got up. It was no use lying in bed imagining myself carrying trays up to Mrs Cartwright for the next ten years and turning gradually into her daughter just when I'd meant to stop being a dutiful daughter here. Soon the sun would be up: the air was fresh and cool. I decided to go up to the cottage for a last look at it. It would never be the same again. I was in a bad temper, angry with everything, angry because I couldn't sleep when I needed to and was tired, angry with the whole world. I laddered a stocking putting it on, then I banged my elbow on the dressing-table. Before going out I made myself a cup of tea and left a tray ready to take up to Mother and Father when I got back – they'll have to get one of those machines after I'm married.

Toby, beastly little dog, heard me moving about and scratched at the study door till I let him out. He's harmless really, I don't know what makes me dislike him so much, there must be some great defect in my character. He yaps so, and he gets so smelly sometimes. Luckily I quite like Tom's Rufus; and anyway he sleeps in a kennel outside and adores Tom so I won't have to bother about him very much. I'm glad Neil hasn't got a dog; Toby would be sure to fight it if he had. When Tom said it was a writer who had rented the cottage I was expecting an 'outsider' person in a fisherman's jersey, or an old man with a beard and cats. He smelt of brandy. He must have been startled when I suddenly appeared. He hadn't been to bed at all, he'd spent the night on the sofa. No wonder, when his bed wasn't made. I'd have done it if I'd known, but then he'd said he wanted to be left alone.

I was frightened all right when he spoke! I hadn't known what to expect when I found the back door open and the kitchen in a shambles. I'd been thinking about Tom and me painting the cottage all the winter, and how much I wanted to live there. Tom and I get on well; he's never cross, one should be glad of that, and he certainly doesn't drink too much, and hardly ever brandy, usually beer. I'd imagined to myself so often what it would be like up there, and how I'd put the pram under the apple tree. Of course the garden down at Combe is lovely, and much bigger, but not the same. Perhaps it's bad luck to imagine about the future like that, perhaps if you do it never happens. That would be dreadful. There's Marjorie with all those children, I'm sure she'd really be happier without any and able to follow up all that culture she worries about. It's funny we're so different, being sisters; she takes after Mother and I'm more like Father, I suppose. It's usually the middle one who's the odd one; Richard's clever too. If I'd been brainy they'd have both been stupid, probably. Oh well, I can cook and knit, and I expect I can learn to cope with calving cows, though as Tom manages all that now I suppose there's no need for me to get mixed up with it; still, the calves are rather sweet; what a pity they're all destined to become beef. There were calves running with their mothers as I crossed the field on the way to the cottage, all the cows had calved by this time; Tom has had some bad nights with them. He was out with one that night when his father was killed. Think of how many times he'd driven home from Chawton before, and then this time he just skidded. The roads were very wet, and then that lorry, and the steering wheel – anyway Mr Cartwright was on the wrong side of the road, it can't have been the lorry driver's fault. You don't stand much chance if you hit a lorry head-on.

I'd got my key out, ready to open the door – we'd kept the spare set of keys and only let the tenant have one, of course. There was the cold tap dripping, drawers open, and a brandy bottle on the sink. I hadn't really got past just being astonished at all that by the time I went into the sitting-room and found the cushions all

higgledy-piggledy and that broken glass on the floor.
Then Toby came in and started rushing about and yapping.

I was horrid to him. It was dreadful of me to kick him:
poor Toby, I can't think what came over me. He was
only being a good watch-dog, after all, but somehow it
was just too much when that bottle went over and spilt.
All the mess and smell; I felt sick with rage. That must
be what people feel like, only more so, who do murders.
I can imagine working yourself up into a passion of
hatred. I suppose if you were brutal enough you'd work
yourself up like that to torture people, like when we
were children and did those awful 'Chinese burns' on
each other's wrists.

Neil was right, it wasn't very pretty, what I did to
Toby. I felt so ashamed; more ashamed because I'd been
seen than because of what I'd done, if the truth were
known. I burn now to think of it. What he must have
thought of me! I had such a shock, turning round to
find him standing on the stairs, though I knew someone
must be there, of course. I didn't think of the tenant; I
was imagining burglars and housebreakers. He looked
so tall, much taller than Tom, and dark; and he has a
sort of mocking way of speaking, as if he were laughing,
but not in a kind way. He was helpless too; he'd forgotten about milk and tea and everything. I came back
home and fetched enough bits and pieces for him to be
going on with. He was nowhere to be seen when I got
back to the cottage, so I put the kettle on and made
coffee. Then he appeared, washed and shaved, a great
improvement. He didn't look very well, but of course he
must have had an awful hangover.

'It's good of you to minister to the interloper,' he said.

I poured him out some coffee.

'I don't suppose you feel like eating an egg,' I said shortly.

He shuddered. 'No, thanks,' he said. 'But this should help.'

'I'll go and see to your bed while you drink it,' I said. 'I don't suppose you know where anything is.'

Before he could stop me, I went off upstairs and got on with getting him straightened up. I had to hurry, as it would soon be time for me to be getting breakfast at home, and I didn't want to go into explanations of where I'd been.

'So domesticated – Mr Cartwright is a fortunate fellow,' said Neil when I came downstairs. I felt that he was laughing at me for being so ordinary.

'We can't all be famous writers,' I said, and began clearing up the kitchen mess.

'I wasn't making comparisons,' Neil said. 'You are in a state today, aren't you? First the dog, and now me.'

'I didn't mean to be rude,' I said at once.

'Calm down,' Neil said. 'You take everything too seriously. Life's a joke, didn't you know?' He came nearer and stared at me. 'It's short. Enjoy it,' he said, and patted my shoulder. 'Come and see me again, Anna, if you can bear to witness the desecration of your love-nest.'

'Oh, it isn't like that,' I muttered crossly. 'You're impossible.'

'Yes, I am. I warned you,' Neil said. He was really laughing at me now, sitting on the corner of the kitchen table. 'Aren't you in love with your Tom? Come now, how shocking!'

'Of course I love Tom,' I said automatically. 'I've known him all my life.'

Neil looked up at the ceiling. 'Heaven preserve us,' he remarked. 'Haven't you ever known any other sort of passion? Anything violent and inexplicable, sweeping you away against your will? No, I suppose you haven't,' and he sighed.

'It sounds much too uncomfortable,' I said stiffly. No one had ever talked to me like this. 'It's not like your book, me and Tom.'

'Your grammar,' said Neil. 'No, I don't suppose it is. So you've read my book, have you? What did you think of it?'

'I loved it, in a queer way,' I told him truthfully. 'I couldn't put it down. And the film was good too. It made me cry. I suppose you've come here to write a book?' I asked, trying to change the subject to something less personal.

'Yes. To finish one,' he said, and turned away. I'd seen bundles of manuscript upstairs among his belongings that were scattered about all over the place.

'I can type,' I said. 'Properly, I mean. I've learnt. If you want any typing done I could help.'

I couldn't think what came over me as I said this. It was so pushing; and anyway, I wasn't sure that I liked Neil or wanted to come up to the cottage while he was there.

'So you haven't been sitting at home like Cinderella waiting for the prince all your life?' Neil said. He was jeering again.

'I went to learn shorthand and typing in London. Then,

just before I finished my training, my sister had a baby
and I had to go and look after her.'

'How inconsiderate of her,' Neil said.

'I didn't mind,' I admitted. 'I hated it in London.'

'And you stayed at home ever afterwards?'

'More or less. I help Dr Fanshawe – he's the local
doctor and lives in the village – sometimes, and I do a
lot of clerical work for my father. We run a market garden,' I said. It sounded very dull, and I felt that Neil
thought so too.

'You help to till the soil?' he asked, and he looked at
my hands. Of course, they were coarse and tanned; I
can never remember to put stuff on them.

'Yes,' I said. 'I quite like it.' It wasn't strictly true.
Sometimes I could scream with the boring monotony of
it, but sometimes that same monotony, all the tasks coming round again annually, is consoling. It's a sort of
security. It will be like that at Combe too, every year the
same: worry about the calves; and the weather; the
harvest, then the ploughing; the ditches to be cleared
and the hedges cut; hay and silage running out; and then
the calves again. I suppose it's like that for most people,
life, I mean. But not for Neil; he must have more excitement. He wouldn't be able to write that sort of book
if he lived a country life all the time, I'm sure.

'So you'll marry your farmer and continue the good
work, and raise a pack of children to carry on,' Neil
said.

'I hope so,' I said coldly. I kept feeling how unsuitable
this conversation was, but I couldn't imagine talking in
any other way to Neil. He wasn't like anybody else; he
was exciting. I felt quite different; awake, and stimu-

lated. I realized how very dull and boring I must seem
to him.

'Well, I might be glad of your help with the manuscript,' Neil said. 'Come up in a day or two and see.'

He didn't say anything about how kind it was of me
to offer, or make any protest. He just accepted it. I suppose if you are celebrated and clever like that, you simply
do just take the rest of the world for granted. Very
haughty.

Tom rang up in the evening. We've hardly seen each
other for the last fortnight. I wondered if he'd telephoned
because he wanted me to write a letter to the Ministry of
Agriculture for him, but he didn't say anything about such
an idea, just chatted. I'm going over to see his mother tomorrow. Tom is very reliable; everyone says so, and of
course I know it too. Marjorie thought I'd never marry
anyone. I wouldn't have, if there hadn't been Tom; I
never meet any men who are old enough, except married ones. But now I've met Neil. I wonder how old he
is? A bit older than Tom, I should think. Tom's forty.
He's getting a bald patch. I suppose in the end he gave
up hoping to meet anyone more exciting than me, too.
At least we know where we are with each other; we
aren't stuffed full with a lot of romantic illusions.
Romance!

'Might as well get hitched up, old girl, what do you
say?' That was how Tom proposed, just as we were packing up the tombola after the church fête last year.

'All right. Good idea,' I said. I'd thought of it, of course,
for ages. Marjorie had teased me about Tom, even
though she never really thought it would come off. I'm
very fond of him; he's a dear, of course. It would be

dreadful if anything happened to him. When I thought he had been in the car with his father that night, I was terrified, but naturally I didn't let him know that, he had enough to cope with, without my adding hysterics to the list. Tom's kind. He'll never let me down, I know that.

Neil isn't kind. His face is hard – sardonic, that's the word. I wonder what his new book's about. His type-writer looked very dusty, but I could use my own if he does want me to work for him.

'Good-bye, Anna,' he said, as I hurried off. 'My bark is worse than my bite. Come back and find out for your-self.'

And of course I shall.

3

Neil

THE village shop in Westington is to me an unusual establishment, but I suppose its replica may be found in most rural areas in England. It is a combined con-fectioner's, bakery and general grocery store, and sells almost everything from frozen fish to reels of thread. It is housed in the front room of a small thatched cot-tage, and anyone as tall as I am must duck his head as he enters, then stand stooping inside. Fortunately for her comfort, the proprietress is short.

Most of the customers are the under-five-year-olds, who do not yet go to school and can therefore be sent upon errands. They arrive, clutching by one hand a still younger brother or sister, and with the other a shopping-bag containing a grubby list of requirements and a well-worn purse. The woman, Mrs Potter, takes charge of list and purse and fills the bag, substituting whatever she thinks fit for any goods that are not in stock. At the end of the list there is authority for the messenger to purchase his wage, usually sherbert fizz or liquorice sticks to the value of threepence. The ritual is becoming familiar to me now since my first morning in Westington. In a way I enjoy watching, and have abandoned my original scheme for shopping by remote control in Chawton. There is something restful in the unhurried way of life that persists here; even the air is calm and mild, and no one is too busy to stop for a moment's conversation. In fact I have not after all wrapped the cloak of a recluse around myself.

Mrs Potter, the shopkeeper, is an obliging soul. She is nearer seventy than sixty; her hair is grey and straggly, drawn into a small bun at the back of her round head. She wears steel-rimmed spectacles behind which bright blue eyes, still unfaded, observe the world with unfaltering shrewdness. Her generous contours are wrapped in a flowered and spotless pinafore, and she wears stubby-heeled laced shoes of the type that I associate with materially distressed ex-governesses. Everything that I require may be bought from Mrs Potter. I expected to eat very little; food had lost importance; but surprisingly my appetite has revived with the exercise involved in walking up and down the hill, and though it tires me, in the long run it cannot matter. The first day that I walked down, there was a small, freckle-faced boy in the shop. He had the unlikely sum of fourpence-halfpenny to spend, and took five minutes to decide how best to lay it out. While I watched Mrs Potter guiding his choice, I leaned against a pile of biscuit tins stacked by the wall, and contemplated conscripting the child as my messenger and delivery boy. He seemed in need of funds. But when he left, clutching a revolting miscellany of gaily coloured sweets, I made no move to enlist him. It amuses me now to watch Mrs Potter serving her clientele: young women, smug sometimes in the plump aftermath of recent maternity; older ones, flat-footed, their bodies spread with time; weather-beaten men in dirty caps and worn clothing, labourers from the farms about; bright-eyed schoolchildren; but chiefly near-infants. Most days I walk down at some time or another. Mrs Potter can instantly, in the fastness of her shop, which is a mass of concealed nooks and corners, find whatever is required. In a recess at the back of the premises gleams the purring white refrigerator. Mrs Potter's plump buttocks are turned towards her customers as she plunges head-first into this cabinet, delving for steakettes, fish fingers and green beans. I sometimes wonder if the children of this country village have ever tasted beef unminced or even vegetables freshly grown in the garden, so much seems to pass across the counter; but most of the cottages have gardens that are cultivated, and later in the year no doubt the demand for frozen greens will cease.

The milkman calls at the cottage. I have warning of his approach each day because of the noise his van makes roaring in low gear up the hill. This gives me time to take refuge away from the doorway so that I do not have to communicate with him. He bangs down my half-pint on the step with a crash that ought to shatter the bottle, whistles his way back down the path, turns his van with a scurry of flints in the roadway, and vanishes at high speed. We meet once weekly face to face, on Saturdays when I pay him, and I have determined that this shall be the limit of our communication.

The middle chapters of the book are drafted out, and it is building up towards the climax, but there is a great deal of work still to do, and I shall use the help of the girl, Anna. She returned, of course, as I knew she would, bringing with her an offering of eggs as a reason for her visit. She seemed apprehensive. However, I resisted the urge to needle her, and she calmed down; I soon learned the rest of her life story. Her father is a retired colonel – axed, I suppose – who runs a market garden; they live in a rather lovely Georgian house screened by trees and a high wall from the village. Even while Colonel Harris was a serving soldier this was their family base, though it was sometimes let. Anna was at a boarding-school in Wales for most of the war, which seems to have touched her very little. Her sister, who is older and clever, is married to a successful advertising executive and lives at Gerrards Cross. Anna thinks of this pair as intellectuals. They have four children, a girl, a twin boy and girl, and another girl. There is also a brother, younger than Anna, who is following in his father's military footsteps. Mother is a J.P. and inclined towards good works. Anna is obviously being rescued by her farmer from a dreary fate as a patient maiden aunt and household drudge. It has been a revelation to me to hear her unfold this history, for I thought such women no longer existed. She was evidently too diffident to insist on spreading her wings when younger, and was glad of the reprieves offered by varying crises where her aid was sought, so that she drifted on until it became too late for her to fly out into the world. She took away a pile of manuscript to type; she will be conscientious to the ultimate limit and return it without one error, I am confident, and the thrill she will get from doing so will be greater than any she has ever known.

She was surprised to find that the cottage was tidy and clean.

'I can be orderly, you see, when I'm sober,' I said. In fact I surprised myself by the pains I was taking to observe some degree of cleanliness and method, but as soon as I had to endure another bad spell I knew it would all be lost.

'Are you comfortable? There's nothing you want?' She glanced round the room.

'I have all I need,' I told her, and at last she could postpone her departure no longer. She went away, promising to return the typed work almost at once.

Anna was not my only visitor, for Cartwright himself looked in the next evening. I'd had a bad day and been at the brandy again. He would not accept the tot I offered him and looked disapprovingly at me as I helped myself, thinking the worst, no doubt, of those who drink alone. I was surprised to find that there was nothing of the yokel about him, in spite of his appearance; he is a burly man, red-faced and with sandy hair going back fast. We found little to discuss, and he left after ten minutes when he had made sure that I was content with the arrangements in the cottage. I shuddered to think of the years of dead conversation that lie ahead for Anna and this man; still, neither is aware that anything else exists. Doubtless they will produce a tribe of equally moronic children, and this is the strain that made England. Well, introspective drunks are of questionable merit too.

That night I had a dream about Fenella. It was so real that when I woke it was difficult to remember where I was, and why, and that I had not seen her for two years. I did not even know if she was still in Australia. She would only feel pitying revulsion if she saw me now; and if I saw her, whatever I felt, it was too late for alteration. The same impulse that made me taunt the girl Anna, and flaunt my drunkenness before Cartwright, had compelled me to goad her beyond the bounds of patience, and Fenella was not able to accept endurance. We tore each other into pieces, meeting occasionally only in bursts of rare joy which were for me enough compensation for the torment in between, but were for her inadequate. The dream unnerved me and I could not write a word all day; I went for a long walk, exhausting myself, and then I went down to the village, hoping that perhaps the sight of Mrs Potter's homely features would help to wipe the image of Fenella from my mind.

As I walked from the shop I met the vicar. He was riding a bicycle down the main street of the village, an old-fashioned, high machine, with the rider balanced upright, a scarf round his thin neck. He pedalled rather wildly past the pond, then saw me, and with screechings and squeaks from his indifferent brakes drew to an unsteady halt and dismounted. He is remarkably thin, far thinner than I am, but not old – fifty, perhaps – with a hearty manner quite out of keeping with his frail appearance.

'Ah, Mr Addington, I am sure you must be he,' he cried enthusiastically.

I nodded in agreement.

'You see, we know all about you in Westington,' he went on. I doubted, but not aloud, whether they did.

'The milkman told me you had arrived, and I had planned to call next week. I am sure you are here to work upon a book, but, nevertheless, I must extract a promise from you.' He lifted an admonitory finger and wagged it at me.

'I'm an agnostic,' I said at once, to forestall him.

'Oh, dear me, Mr Addington, you don't expect me to believe that, do you?' he cried archly. 'Not after reading *The Breakers*? Why, belief shines through every word – unacknowledged, maybe, but present. Very much so.'

I was taken aback, not so much by this allegation as by the fact that he had read my book, which was not one likely to reach an ecclesiastical household.

'Your thinking is muddled, of course, and I'm looking forward to a chat when you've an hour to spare,' the vicar went on keenly. 'I'm sure we'd have a most stimulating discussion. But first I want to enlist your support. I want you to open our church fête next month. June the twenty-ninth at three o'clock in the vicarage garden.'

'I'm not a suitable person. I shall never come to church,' I said defensively, unable to think of a better excuse immediately. I intended to speak brusquely, but the words sounded mild as I uttered them.

'My dear fellow, you're a celebrity, a "personality", in fact; as if we are not all "personalities" in our way, however humble. You have even, if I am not mistaken, appeared upon the television, so that those who have not read your books are none the less familiar with your features. You will be a draw. The end justifies the means in such a case. Besides, most of the money will be given to the Fabric Fund, and I am sure you are in favour of the maintenance of such a lovely and historic building as our little church. You've been inside?'

I shook my head.

'Then I must show you round it,' he declared. 'Part of it is Saxon, but the tower is Norman, as you can see for yourself.' He gestured in the direction of the church, which I had noticed before, grey among the trees. 'You agree, then. June the twenty-ninth. I'll remind you.'

I felt unable to combat his enthusiasm, and nodded.

'Good, that's settled, then,' he said happily, preparing to mount his bicycle once more. 'The committee will be delighted when I tell them you've consented – and by doing so you've already won ten shillings for the good cause.'

'What can you mean?' I asked.

'I had a bet that you'd agree. Tom Cartwright, your landlord – you've met him, I believe – didn't think you would. We arranged that if I was correct he would contribute an extra ten shillings to the kitty.'

'And if I hadn't?' I asked. 'What was your stake?'

'Oh, I'd have done the same,' he said. 'The fund stood to win whatever happened. But I was quite happy about my money, I was betting on a certainty.'

I was left standing in the road, staring after him, clasp-

ing my loaf of brown bread, wondering what made him
so sure; and obscurely irritated because Cartwright had
been confident of my refusal.

4

Letters

PART of Mrs Harris's weekly letter to her daughter
Marjorie:

*. . . I'm glad to hear the twins went back happily to
school. They're sure to do well, they're clever, just like
you and Richard were at that age, and they must get
accustomed to being parted, like ordinary brothers and
sisters, even though their relationship is so much closer.
Don't worry about Lalage, she's at an awkward stage and
it will pass. It's odd, though, how children will sometimes resemble an aunt or uncle more than a parent.*

*Anna has been causing me some anxiety. She seemed
very shocked when Bob Cartwright was killed – of course
it was a terrible tragedy, though fortunate in that he can
have known almost nothing about it, and Elsie's illness
is a pathetic direct result. But at Anna's age one should
have acquired more resilience. The business of letting the
cottage upset her. Mr Foster, the agent in Chawton, had
been approached from someone in London wanting to
find a secluded hide-out for this writer, and as he knew
Tom and Anna's plans had been changed he got in touch
with Tom to see if he would let. It's sensible. They'll*

never live there; Elsie is unlikely to, either, she seems increasingly frail and of course it is a heavy anxiety for poor Tom, especially coming on top of the other. Anna is really not much help to him, but I doubt if it would have made any difference in that direction if they had gone forward with their plans as arranged. In any event it would not have been fair on Elsie, it's not as though poor Anna were gifted with tact; she will be very inept, I fear, as mistress of Combe, but time will improve her. She is fortunate in Tom; I had begun to wonder if he ever would marry her after all, he could manage very well with a housekeeper and he's been a bachelor for so long. Anna is a dear, good girl, but not one calculated to attract. She will be an excellent mother – look how she adores your Lally. She and Tom will probably be content, and that is more than can be said for many. She has been very irritable and jumpy lately, and taken to hiding herself away in her bedroom; goodness knows what she does up there, once I heard her typewriter going hard. As a matter of fact she's doing some typing for this writer man who's got the cottage, but she was banging away before then. I don't suppose she can be writing a novel herself, poor Anna! Perhaps I should speak to her and see if she and Tom can make plans for a new date for the wedding; the postponement may have been too much for her, but Tom could hardly take time off now with the spring sowing and all his father's affairs to settle single-handed.

But you'll be wanting to know how Westington reacts to the writer in our midst. There's been quite a run on his book, the public library in Chawton has got an extra copy, and what a sordid story it is, though undeniably clever. Personally I maintain that the lids should not be lifted off sewers – we all know they exist, but why describe them?

He must be a very odd man. He gave strict orders that he should be left strictly alone, he doesn't even have anyone in to do for him, though Maggie Potter's sister would have gone up willingly enough, in spite of the climb. Heaven knows what condition the place will get into, though the vicar was up there last Friday and he reported that it was spick and span. I wonder he was allowed in, since Mr Addington is so intent on seclusion. He is probably much too conceited to realize that Westington is not the sort of place where a man like himself would be lionized.

He is very tall and cadaverous-looking – there's no other word to describe him. He will not be an asset to us so it's as well he isn't a permanency. He calls frequently at The Grapes and carries away a hold-all 'full of spirits' according to Daisy McBean who works in the bar and is 'going steady' with Joe Finch, your father's new gardener. He doesn't go to church – though it would have been a surprise if he did – but strangely enough the vicar seems to like him, even to approve. It was he who introduced us, in fact. We met in the Post Office, when I was sending you that parcel of shirts for the twins that I bought in Furlough's closing-down sale in Chawton last week. In came the vicar to buy stamps, and then Mr Addington with what must have been an instalment of his book. The vicar made one of his usual tiresome waggish remarks about it. Mr Addington had seemed about to turn and take flight at sight of me, but with ill grace he succumbed enough to let the vicar do the

honours. I felt obliged to make a show of friendliness –
after all it isn't for long, and he is going to open the fête
which will draw people from the district, you know what
they're like. So I asked him round on Saturday evening.
He accepted, rather to my astonishment, as I expected
him to say he must deliver another chapter or whatever
they do, but I suppose he wouldn't turn down a free
drink. I asked the vicar too, of course, and Mrs Gowberry,
and the Fanshawes to help out. Tom couldn't come, he
was too busy.

Anna actually put on a dress, that green one with the
pleated skirt, not a very fortunate choice, perhaps, but
at least she made an effort and didn't walk straight in
from the garden with earth under her fingernails, which
has happened. Mr Addington and the vicar argued for
some time about a theological point that eludes me. Mr
A. seemed curiously well-informed and the vicar was
obviously enjoying their conversation until I broke it
up, fearing it would grow too heated. Dr Fanshawe had
to leave as he was called out to an emergency, nurse
admitting defeat with a difficult baby I imagine, but
Betty stayed. She couldn't make much headway with
Addington – he gave up after talking to the vicar and
simply poured your father's whisky down his throat,
glowering. In fact I think he was several up on the rest
of us when he arrived here, he had that ponderous look
of concentration in his eye. He didn't like Toby, who
came sniffing round him suspiciously – it was mutual,
I suspect, and one always mistrusts a man that dogs
dislike, and who dislikes dogs. He'd seen Toby before,
he told Anna he's seen her out walking with him. It
surprised me, for Anna is not much given to walks, and

not likely to think of taking Toby if she goes over to
Combe. She blushed when he spoke to her, like any
schoolgirl. Really I should have made her go away from
home and learn to mix more easily, but she seemed
happy enough here and there was always plenty to
occupy her. I didn't want to drive her away, and she
didn't enjoy being in London while she trained; besides,
your father said, 'Let her stay.'

'Do you like dogs?' Mr Addington asked her. What a
question!

'Of course she does,' I replied, quite crossly. 'We all
do. Don't you?' And he had the temerity to admit that
he did not, and to imply that dog-lovers were abnormal.
He had quite definitely had too much to drink when he
left; your father was over-hospitable. He went abruptly,
without a word of thanks, leaving us all thunderstruck
at such lack of manners. The vicar, charitable as ever,
made excuses for him and said he had been ill, then he
hurried after him to insist on driving him home. I suppose he was afraid he was incapable of getting there.
He came back quite soon for Mrs Gowberry, but wouldn't
be drawn to speak about the journey.

But I'm sorry Mr Addington discovered Anna could
type. She goes up there to collect the work and deliver
what she's done. I suppose they met again in the village
and he found out, she never mentioned it that evening.
I'm not sure it's a good thing for her to have anything
to do with a man of that sort – judging by his book he
can have no morals at all – but she'll be safe enough, I
suppose, she wouldn't appeal to him.

I had an interesting case in court the other day, to
change the subject which has been the dominant one of

*this letter. It was a boy of sixteen who had run away
from home and been caught stealing. It seemed he felt
unwanted at home, and ill-used; it's sad how badly some
parents fail to understand their children . . .*

Extract from Anna's letter to her niece Lalage:

*. . . The pony idea is splendid, but if it doesn't come
off couldn't you save up for rides at Miss Toynbee's? She
has some good ponies, and it might be difficult for Daddy
and Mummy to manage one for you, especially as you're
the only one who's keen, it would be better value if you
all rode. You might be able to earn some extra rides by
working for Miss Toynbee, cleaning tack and so on, and
you could ask for money for all your presents in future,
at birthday and Christmas.*

*What a blight about the algebra; I could never under-
stand it either, still, the extra lessons will help you to
sort it out and you'll have to bear it till you've done your
G.C.E., it would be too shaming not to take maths. You'll
be able to chuck it later and never think of it again.*

*There isn't much news here. Tom is very busy. There
are lots of new calves and they are rather sweet. Mrs
Cartwright doesn't seem to be any better, she just lies
in bed all day looking out of the window. When it gets
warmer she may improve. Grandfather and I have been
doing lots of hard work planting peas and beans and
things, and Toby has been chasing rabbits – a few have
come back. The next excitement is the church fête at the
end of June, I suppose as usual I'll be doing the produce
stall, though last year Mrs Fanshawe did and I helped
Tom with the tombola. It would be fun if you could*

*come and help, we'll have to see if Mummy will let you
stay that week-end.*

*The cottage has been let, as Tom and I won't be living
there now. A writer called Neil Addington has rented it.
He's rather famous, he wrote that book* The Breakers
*which was made into a film, but I don't suppose you saw
it, it's not the sort of thing you'd like, rather sad, about a
boy belonging to one of those awful gangs in London,
and in the end he died – the boy I mean. Mr Addington
has come here to write another book, and as it has to be
finished by a certain date I am helping him by typing
out the manuscript. It's much more fun than doing
Grandfather's accounts . . .*

5

Anna

WHEN Mother came in from the village and said she'd
asked Neil round for a drink I could have sunk through
the floor! It wasn't just because I was surprised that she'd
asked him, it was also amazement that he'd accepted, as
he seemed so determined to keep out of village life. I
said nothing then about having already met him, and
afterwards of course it was too late. If you don't admit
something like that right at the beginning it's always too
difficult or impossible to put it right afterwards and you
have to embark on a path of deceit.

The evening was dreadful. Luckily Mother had also
asked the Gowberrys and the Fanshawes, so it didn't

matter me being dumb as usual. Betty F. talks enough for three, but she didn't do very well with Neil, he didn't seem to enjoy her wit. He liked the vicar, though, they argued for ages, quite good-naturedly, Neil didn't get that black look on his face till after Mother had dragged him away from Mr Gowberry. It always seems to me to be a pity to disrupt people at parties who are enjoying themselves in an effort to make them circulate. Still, it's bad luck to be stuck all evening with a dead weight, of course, so it cuts both ways.

Betty Fanshawe was as gay as a cricket. She had on such a pretty pink dress, she looked far too young to have five children. Pam will be home for half-term the week-end of the fête, so if Lally comes she'll probably give her a few rides; in fact they could both do the pony rides for the fête as well, which would be a good excuse to get Lal down.

Neil hadn't changed, he just came in flannels and a jacket, but with a tie, luckily. Mother wouldn't have cared for that cravat arrangement he often wears. He is thin; the back of his neck, below the hair line, is so thin that there are hollows in it on each side, like an old man. Men's necks are usually so solid-looking, once they've passed the scraggy stage and filled out. Tom's is hard and thick; and the back of Hugh's neck looks like a stubborn tree-trunk, I should hate to keep looking at it, like Marjorie must have to do. Perhaps she doesn't see his back view much.

Mother wore her grey, which meant she was feeling very formal. Father changed too, he said it was because the vicar was coming, but really I think they were all a bit conscious of the fact that they were entertaining a celebrity whose views were not their own, and they were being super-conventional as a defence. I put on my old green, it doesn't really suit me but it's the best I've got. I suppose I'll have to get some new things for when I'm married, not that Tom ever seems to notice and we won't be going to any more smart occasions than we do now, just the same old round as usual. In a way I was glad he didn't come that night; he'd already said he'd been up to see Neil, and I knew he hadn't liked him, though he never said so. I didn't say I'd met him too, so as well as not saying it to the parents, I've also pretended about it to Tom, which is far worse. Tom would never lie to me; now I've acted a lie, by omission, to him. If he'd been there that evening he would have noticed something when Neil talked about Toby. Anyway, apart from me, why didn't Neil say we'd met already? He pretended, too. And then he challenged Mother about dog-lovers! It's bad enough to challenge her about anything, but choosing dogs as the subject is about the worst you could pick on. Fancy having the nerve to tell her that dog-lovers inflict their animals on everyone else and expect them to enjoy being sniffed at and clawed, licked, or even nipped. I was sure there would be a row, but luckily Mr Gowberry intervened by asking Neil what he meant by something in his book. Even so, he left very abruptly, and without saying any sort of thank-you. He'd gone rather pale, paler than usual, that is; I wouldn't admit it to anyone except myself, but I'm afraid he'd drunk too much again. Practically the only things he seems to put in the dustbin at the cottage are empty bottles. Once, when he was in a good mood and not trying to pick a quarrel with me, I told him he should try and drink less, and he flew into a towering rage. He said if I knew what he knew I'd drink too. He frightened me, but I asked him what he meant.

'Oh, if you had my knowledge of people, of life, death and the fates,' he cried, and then went ranting on about people's motives for their actions. I didn't understand a word; I'm not at all sure he was talking sense anyway. His new book is so odd in patches that I'm not certain if it makes sense either; anyway it's very hard to believe that people behave the way Neil's characters do. It's a compelling story, you want to know what happens, and you can't help feeling sorry for the hero who's in an awful mess with blackmail and two women and goodness knows what else, but he brought it all on himself of course. Neil says it's allegorical, and that it won't end happily because things don't. He must have been very unhappy all his life himself, he never seems to think that people can be kind just because they're nice, he always thinks there's some ulterior motive, and that everyone's beastly under the polite social surface. Anyway he seems pleased with the typing I've done, I took great care with it and didn't make any mistakes. He says time is precious and he wants to get it done as soon as possible. Already I'm getting used to his scribbly handwriting and can read it fairly easily. My spelling isn't too reliable so I use the dictionary a good deal when I'm not sure of a word.

After he'd flown off the handle to me about this great burden of knowledge that was weighing him down, he flopped on to the sofa and said, 'Anyway, I've no future. Fame for a week and then no more.'

I could have shaken him for being so ungrateful.

'You've been famous for years, and you'll be better thought of than ever after this book comes out,' I said.

'Even people who can't agree with you respect your opinions, like Mr Gowberry.'

'I respect his too,' he said then. He leaned forward suddenly and put his hands over his eyes. I was afraid he felt ill; he hadn't been drinking I knew, otherwise I wouldn't have dared argue with him. All at once he jumped up, swore dreadfully in words I'd never even heard of, and told me to go away. He stood there, waiting, looming, while I tried to keep calm and collect up his papers to carry away; I suppose I was nearly crying, I was certainly frightened of his temper. I hurried off towards the kitchen as I always go up over the fields and through the garden, and just as I was going out of the back door he called me back.

'Anna!'

I looked round, almost deciding to pretend I hadn't heard, and he did that queer smile of his that looks as if it hurts him, it is so reluctant and so rare.

'Come back,' he said. He didn't say he was sorry; he could never apologize, but I knew that if he could, he would. I came back across the kitchen towards him, and he gave a funny little shrug.

'Let's put on a record,' he said. He'd brought a record player. So we went back into the sitting-room and he played me a Mozart symphony. It was lovely. We just sat there quietly, listening, and then I went away. He asked me to stay and cook him some supper, and share it, but I couldn't because I had to get it at home, so he said that I must stay the next time I came up, and I agreed.

When I got home Father was moving the sprinkler. It had been on the lettuces all day, we'd had such a long spell of fine weather that everything had got very dry. I went to help, first of all putting down the bundle of manuscript.

'What's that you've got?' Father asked, looking at the package.

'A bit more of Neil's book,' I answered, without thinking. Then I realized I hadn't said 'Mr Addington'. I don't know whether Father noticed, or if he would have paid any attention anyway; sometimes I wonder if he ever notices anything except his plants and his seedlings, but at other times I'm not sure that much escapes him. He never says much, but he's always worth hearing. He must be rather lonely, he and Mother hardly ever seem to communicate. Perhaps if you've been married long enough you never need to talk, or perhaps you just don't want to any more. It's depressing to think about, but silence is better than rows, like Marjorie and Hugh have when he comes home tired, and she's feeling chatty and wants to be made a fuss of, and he won't be bothered; but they're happy really; they're almost too wordy, the way they dissect everything in conversation.

Father said then, when he'd finished rearranging the sprinkler, 'Did you meet Tom? He was down here looking for you about half an hour ago. Wanted to take you to the cinema. He said you hadn't had an evening out together for a long time, and there's a good film on in Chawton. Why don't you ring him up? There's still time.'

I wasn't very sure that I wanted to see Tom just then.

'I've done nothing about supper yet,' I said, temporizing.

'We'll open some tins. I'll be chef,' said Father. 'Old Tom hasn't seen much of you since you've been spending all your spare time working for Addington.'

I felt guilty. 'I couldn't refuse to help him, when he asked me,' I protested. 'It isn't for long.'

'You know your own business, Anna my dear,' said Father. 'But don't forget Tom.'

'Mr Addington wants to get the book finished by the end of July, he's promised the publisher,' I said, defiantly. I felt that Father was criticizing me, and I felt too that he was justified.

'It's your affair, my dear,' Father said. He began to walk away up the garden. 'But take my advice and go to that film with Tom.'

My head was full of whirling impressions of the afternoon up at the cottage and Neil's violent changes of mood. The cinema was the last place that I wanted to be in; I'd planned to get the latest pages of the new book typed that night. But Father was right; I'd scarcely given Tom a thought for days and that afternoon I'd completely forgotten his existence.

When he answered the telephone his voice sounded impatient.

'Father told me you wanted to go to the cinema,' I said.

'It's that good film about Africa that you wanted to see, I thought you'd enjoy it,' he replied.

'Yes, I would, but not if you don't want to,' I said.

'We haven't been anywhere for ages,' Tom said. 'I got finished early today, so I came down. I've hardly seen you for the past month.' I couldn't be sure if it was just imagination that made me think his voice sounded accusing, or whether it was my own bad conscience making me think it.

'I'm sorry,' I said, rather stiffly. 'I'd like to go to the cinema, but don't feel you've got to take me.'

'Oh, hell, Anna, you know I want to see you,' he said angrily. 'I'll be round in ten minutes.' And he rang off.

Tom hadn't spoken to me like that since he blew his top four years ago when Marjorie left one of his gates unlatched and the cattle got out into the wheat. I didn't have time to speculate about it; I flew upstairs, put the manuscript safely away and had just time to powder my nose and comb my hair before he arrived. I went out by the back door; Father was in the kitchen busy with his cooking, adding tomatoes and grated cheese to a tin of ravioli. I praised his initiative, and he said he'd have to learn to get handier when I'm married. Then he kissed me, something he rarely does.

'Enjoy yourself this evening. You look very nice,' he said.

It couldn't be true. I looked the same as usual, except rather red in the face from all the sun we've had lately, but it was kind of him to say it, all the same.

I was out in the drive before Tom had finished turning the car. Even so, he got out to see me into it. I wonder how long he'll go on doing that sort of thing and letting me go first through doors after we're married. Father has wonderful manners, of course, but a lot of men haven't. Neil's are not good; but a lot is due to environment and upbringing, so it isn't fair to make comparisons.

Tom kissed me, too, of course, briskly, and he gave me one of those odd little hugs that are rather nice and comforting.

'I'm sorry I was such a bear,' he said. 'I'd given you up and started clearing out my desk.'

'We don't have to go. I'll come and help with the desk,' I said.

'It'll keep,' he said. 'We're going out, on our own, and after the flick we're having a good feed at the Bell and Anchor. I hope you're hungry, I've rung them up and ordered scampi and steak. I'm ravenous myself already.'

'Didn't you have any tea?' I asked.

'I forgot about it,' Tom said. 'But I did have a piece of cake off Mother's tray.'

By now we had left Westington and were on the main road into Chawton. There wasn't much traffic about, and Tom, as he sometimes did, took his left hand from the wheel and held it out towards me. As I took it, I had a sudden urge to press it as hard as I could with both mine, almost to hurt him. Such a wild feeling frightened me. Naturally I did nothing of the sort, and just held it in the normal gentle way, and I soon calmed down.

The film was good, and I enjoyed it. We hadn't been to the cinema since Tom's father died; we used to go, during the winter, about once a month, when there was anything on worth seeing. We held hands again during the film, and I was happy with Tom's bulky arm resting against my shoulder. While we had dinner he told me about the various things he'd been doing at the farm, and how there was a chance that he might be able to buy that big field that runs into the middle of Combe Farm almost cutting it in two. When we got home he came in for a whisky and soda with Father. Even though it was late they were still up; Mother had been dealing with her British Legion minutes, she's the secretary now. Father was reading *Death in the Dairy*. I went out with Tom when he left. It was a fine, mild night, with half a moon and just a few clouds drifting above the trees.

'We mustn't get so snowed under with our work that we forget to see each other, Annie,' he said, putting his arms round me to give me his good-night kiss. He often calls me Annie; no one else ever does, and I wouldn't like them to. Suddenly I felt like I had done in the car. I clung to him in a silly way, and pressed my face into his jacket shoulder. He held me more tightly and stroked my hair, not saying anything, dismayed, I should think, by my wild behaviour. When I eventually looked up at him it was hard to see his face in the pale light of the moon. I felt that I could not bear to let him go.

'Let's get married soon, Tom. Why are we putting it off?' My voice sounded fierce and muttering, not at all like it does as a rule. 'We're neither of us young. There's no need for a lot of fuss. We could just get married very quietly. Let's.'

'Darling, we can't for a little while,' he said, stroking my hair again. 'We must give Mother time to get a little stronger. And besides, your mother will expect to have a bit of a do.'

'Well, she can do without it,' I said. 'I should think she'd be glad to get me off her hands at last,' I went on bitterly, drawing away from him. 'Can't we fix a date, at least, Tom? Next month?'

'Annie, I don't see how we can,' Tom said. 'We don't know what's going to happen. And then there's the hay.'

'Oh, blow the hay,' I cried. 'That's just an excuse. We needn't go away, I could just move in to Combe. You obviously don't want us to get married after all.' I could feel that beastly lump in my throat that meant I was going to cry.

'Annie, darling, I want us to be married more than I've ever wanted anything else in the world,' Tom said. 'But what are a few weeks – months even – to us when they may make all the difference in the world to Mother? When she starts to pick up we'll fix the first date that we can.'

'It'll be harvest then,' I said sulkily. 'You'll be too busy.'

'I won't, Annie. I can leave things to Bryce and lay on extra help,' Tom said. 'By September we should see how things are going to be, darling. I know it isn't always easy for you at home, but be patient, there's a dear girl. It isn't very long.'

I thought, no, it isn't very long, but it's as long as Neil will be in Westington, and I was afraid.

6

Neil

THERE is a curious balm about life in this village; like a soporific, the slow pace of the days, the quiet air, the absence of hustle and stress are affecting me, and I am even finding it hard to maintain, in the book, the aggressive drive of my theme. Westington is still a backwater: the young go to work by bus or motor-cycle in Chawton's shops or single factory; the older ones work on the land. But new houses are to be built, and overflows from neighbouring towns are coming this way; Chawton is to grow, and I wonder how much longer the calm tenor of village existence will continue.

Anna has told me some of the less obvious excitements which lurk beneath the surface; and sometimes, in The Grapes, when I call for my supplies, I learn of others. Here, everyone is known: that is the dominating fact which is so different from life in cities. As the village grows larger this feature may be lost, but at present all here are known if not by sight at least by reputation. Already I have learned at second hand the history of Mrs Watts and her adopted family of three sons: they were East End children evacuated to Westington during the war; afterwards they returned to live with her rather than go back to their own squalid home and wrangling parents, and now that she is old and frail, they, all married, vie with each other in the matter of caring for her – although she insists still on maintaining as much independence as she can. At the other end of the scale there is a family who spends most of its time in prison or in Borstal, though theft and violence are rare in Westington; the lawbreaking part of the community commits most of its misdeeds elsewhere.

One day a leak developed in the overhead cistern at the cottage, and I was forced to seek out Cartwright for aid. I walked over the big field, gingerly avoiding the cows, to Combe Farm, which lies at the bottom of the slope sheltered behind a row of stately elms. The house is old and attractive; I had not expected that. It is large and square, built of brick and painted cream, with roses climbing all over the front of it, and a yard and outbuildings at the side. A black labrador lay on the threshold of the open front door; when I approached he got slowly to his feet and began waving his powerful tail to and fro. Unlike the small yapping Toby, Anna's encumbrance, he did not repel me, and I felt constrained to pat his large head in a tentative manner, at the same time reflecting that his friendly greeting showed him to have no value as a watch-dog. I rang the bell, and very soon a hospital nurse in uniform appeared.

I remembered that Cartwright's mother was an invalid; this, her attendant, was a muscular woman with a kind, capable expression on her face, but I already disliked her because of the associations her profession had for me. My errand, however, was urgent, if the kitchen ceiling was not to join the growing pool of water on the floor; and though I felt no qualms about the hardship Cartwright would face through meeting, as in the terms of the lease, the cost of repair, I did not want the inconvenience of workmen in the cottage for longer than could be helped.

In answer to my query, the nurse told me that Cartwright was hay-making, and she directed me towards the field where I might find him. I set off to track him down, helped by the distant sound of tractor engines. It was hot, and I hurried; by the time I reached him, at the farther end of a twenty-acre field, I was tired. Wearing a faded shirt and shabby trousers, Cartwright was driving a tractor that towed a machine making the hay into neat bundles and throwing them clear, back to the ground. It was intriguing to watch; I had plenty of time to study the process as I walked over the close-cut grass. Another man pulled a giant rake around, gathering up the hay into lines ready for the baler; he saw me coming and gestured to his employer, who turned and waved, then jumped down from his tractor to come and meet me. I could imagine that the interruption I made was as infuriating to him as I should have found his sudden eruption into a room where I was writing. However, he greeted me with civility, and above the noise of the tractor's engine I shouted the explanation for my presence. He nodded, evidently having heard, retraced his steps to turn off the machinery, and then set forth back towards the farmhouse. I had difficulty in keeping pace with his long strides; he was a fit and muscular man, and I was a wreck. I hated him for his strength.

At the house he said: 'Of course you turned the water off at the main.'

I had to confess that such a thought had not occurred to me, though even if it had I would have had no idea where to find the stopcock. I said so, hoping to imply by my tone that it was a reflection on him as a landlord not to have provided me with this information. 'I left a tap running,' I added.

'Hm; a few more minutes won't make much difference, I suppose,' said Cartwright, more or less to himself. He went into the house and picked up the telephone.

'It's dripping quite slowly,' I said, in mitigation, while he nodded and got on with the business of communicating with the plumber.

'He's out, but he'll be given a message,' Cartwright said. 'I'd better go up and turn off the main meanwhile. It'll do no more damage then.' He spoke with the controlled courtesy of one who longed to be rude, and I wondered why it was that he disliked me so much; it was not just because I was obviously impractical and incompetent in fields where he excelled; and so far I had proved to be an obedient tenant, paying my rent regularly and even, with Anna's assistance (of which I was sure he was unaware), maintaining his property in a fair degree of order. By now, however, I felt so dizzy and exhausted that I was incapable of walking the short distance up the hill once more.

'Do you mind if I rest for a minute?' I asked, sitting down quickly on a chair in the hall, before I fell. 'I've been ill, and walking fast tires me.' Thus I hoped to make him feel responsible for my collapse because of the brisk pace he had maintained; I was not too far gone to try this provocation.

He peered at me, and an expression of reluctant concern replaced the frown he had worn. 'You do look rather green,' he remarked. 'I'll fetch you some brandy.'

He disappeared, and soon returned carrying a glass. He stood over me while I drank it, with the manner of a child angrily having to minister to the welfare of a weaker but unworthy junior.

'You go and see to the water; I'll be all right in a minute,' I said, conscious of his impatience. He went away again, without answering, and this time returned with the nurse, who at once surrounded me with her aura of professionalism. Cartwright left me in her charge, saying that he would take me back in the car when I had recovered. I was then forced to surrender weakly to her. She led me to a large and comfortable sofa in a pleasant, rather shabby room, where I was only too thankful to obey her instructions to lie down. She took my pulse and looked at me penetratingly, but I would not be drawn into divulging the details of my illness, though I did admit that I had not been out of hospital for very long.

I added, rather truculently, that my heart was all right, and that I would soon feel better.

When Cartwright returned I had almost decided to walk back to the cottage without waiting for him, but in fact I was glad to submit and accept his offer of transport. First, he said that he must send down to the hayfield to let the men know he was still detained and to arrange for the work to go on without him. Before leaving, he gave me another brandy, for which I was grateful. Nurse Thomson meanwhile came back into the room, and seeing that I had recovered suggested that I should make the acquaintance of Mrs Cartwright while I waited.

'Provided you can manage the stairs,' she added.

'Of course I can manage the stairs,' I said testily. Her challenge compelled me to take it up, though I had no wish to meet Mrs Cartwright and would have done much to avoid entering any sick-room.

'It might cheer her up to see a new face,' Nurse told me as I followed her starched rear up the stairs. 'Poor dear, we're not able to rouse her much. She speaks very little, though she seems to appreciate what's said to her. She hasn't got over the shock.'

I had not realized that Mrs Cartwright was almost helpless. She lay propped up on pillows in a large four-poster bed hung with sprigged drapes. Wide windows were open to the garden, and the air was full of the scent of roses and sweet peas, which were arranged in bowls round the room. The scene was cheerful and sunlit, but the chief character in the drama being waged was reaching the end of her role. As I looked at her pale, transparent face I knew it.

She turned her head very slowly to look at me, incuri-

ously. Nurse, in a bright voice, was busy introducing us
and explaining my presence in the house. She said that
I too had just been ill, but look how I was now picking
up, able to walk in the fields and write my books, and
so would she pick up in no time at all.

The sick woman stared at me. Her eyes seemed very
large in the pallor of her face: steadily we regarded one
another, and for both there was recognition. She nodded
very slightly. I sat down on the chair Nurse had drawn
forward, and I heard my own voice inquire: 'Would you
like me to read to you sometimes? It helps to pass the
time when the days are long.' She nodded again, and I
told her I would bring some poetry to read. She lifted
her hand very slightly, and a fleeting smile touched her
features.

'We like a nice read, don't we?' Nurse said heartily.
'Something cheerful, that's the ticket.'

I could sense the inward shudder Mrs Cartwright felt.
Nurse rattled on gaily; her fund of inane small talk was
inexhaustible, and while I acknowledged her undeniable
good nature and worth, I despised her. So, I suspected,
did her patient.

Cartwright soon returned, and when she heard him
moving about below, Nurse led me away.

'Mr Addington's done your mother such a lot of good,'
she enthused. 'She really took an interest, and he's going
to come and read to her. Such a kindness. She hardly ever
lets me; she knows how little time I have, dear soul.'

I thought that Mrs Cartwright might have other reasons for her reluctance.

'Good of you,' said Cartwright shortly. 'I'm sure you
haven't the time, either.'

I was sure too; I could not analyse the motives that had made me volunteer to undertake a task that would be a burden and from which I would myself derive no advantage; I knew only that I was compelled by the invisible affinity between two afflicted people.

'I'd be glad to help her,' I said, and it was true. 'I won't pass out on you again. I'm all right if I avoid haste.'

'You shouldn't be living alone if you're liable to fainting spells,' Nurse said chidingly. She began to speculate as to when I had last seen the doctor and whether I ate enough protein.

'I'm perfectly well. I just can't go for five-mile walks,' I said irritably.

Cartwright, clearly impatient to be rid of me, chivvied me off towards the car which was now standing out in the yard. We drove in silence up the hill; he was busy thinking: I could almost hear the machinery moving in his head. Finally he gave utterance to his thoughts.

'You ought to have the telephone, you know,' he said. 'In case you feel ill. Nurse was right. But I'm afraid it isn't easy to get it laid on; there's such a demand. I had trouble in fixing it for my bailiff.'

'There's nothing wrong with me that can't be relieved with brandy, as I'm sure you've realized,' I said ungraciously.

'Maybe not. All the same, I propose to fit you up with some sort of alarm system,' Cartwright said. 'I could rig up an electric bell connected with the farm. With my mother ill there's always someone in the house, and the distance across the fields isn't very great. You could ring it if you needed help. After all, you are my tenant and I don't want any trouble.'

As he said this I had the impression that he was not speaking only of my health, though a sense of duty that was to me incomprehensible was behind his words.

'If it will reassure you, please do whatever you like,' I said, trying to keep the belligerent tone out of my voice.

He nodded brusquely. Already, however unwillingly, our lives were inextricably involved. Without alluding again to the action he proposed, he showed me where the water main was, and for good measure the electricity switch and fuse-box. Then he left.

I watched him go. No feeling of mutual regard had drawn us together; we were, in fact, hostile: but each now recognized the other's very different merit, and each was committed indirectly to aid the other, and so to assume an unwelcome responsibility.

7

Anna

As usual at this time of the year, everything is dated by its relation to the fête. 'I can't possibly do that before the fête,' is a reason for refusing an unwelcome task or invitation, or, 'That's before the fête, I'll just manage it,' for the reverse. Lists are being made and discarded, plans laid and countermanded, and merchandise obtained by every method. As often in the past, I'm landed with the produce stall, but that means I get off lightly and am spared having to scrounge, since nearly everything can be supplied from the garden. Tom is running the bottle tombola again. This works well since he can get a lot of bottles on a sale-or-return basis from the pub, but poor Tom once again has to produce a bottle of whisky himself plus a few other star attractions, and as he hates begging he'll end up stocking it nearly single-handed. Father has given him some not very good sherry, and the Fanshawes produced two bottles of port. I told Neil he ought to surrender one of his many bottles of brandy. It would do much more good to the Fabric Fund than to him, I said, and he answered that it was all a question of relative values. I couldn't understand him, but I didn't want to make him angry so I didn't ask him to explain. This conversation took place when I stayed at the cottage for supper.

I'd taken up the middle chapters of the book, all typed and checked. He glanced through them: he always alters things in a most annoying way when the manuscript is so neat and clean. Sometimes I have to type out whole pages again while he walks up and down behind me, muttering and smoking, and scribbling all over the next few sheets. But I must admit that his changes are always improvements. It's rather exciting watching the book grow. First there are only a few characters, then gradually more become involved, and a chain of events develops leading them up to a climax. I can't see how it's all going to end except that I know it will be tragic.

Neil gets very impatient while I type out the pages again, and I'm slow because I'm afraid of making mistakes with him stalking about the room. We argued about how to spell 'desperate'; I was sure it had two 'a's' like 'separate', but of course Neil was right and it hadn't; it was very stupid of me to differ from him. He got into a furious rage and called me a silly, ignorant fool with no education. I felt rather sick and frightened sitting there at the table with the typewriter in front of me while he fumed. I tried to keep on typing, watching the words appear on the roller and pretending not to hear. I knew it was only one of his moods; he has got a vile temper, but he can't help it, and anyway he was right, I am stupid, foolish, ignorant and uneducated. Eventually he went out of the room to get a drink and when he came back the storm was over; he carried on as if nothing had happened, but it took me a little time to get over the shakes which I always seem to develop when he's angry.

After I'd finished the typing he gave me the new bit to take home; it was even more scribbly than usual, he must have found it hard to write, there are so many crossings-out. He explained about various bits that had to be added in, in the middle. Then he said: 'What shall we have for supper?'

I'd expected him to forget, though I'd warned Mother that I'd be out. She said: 'Oh yes, Anna, do go up to Combe. It will be nice for you. Give Elsie my love,' and I didn't tell her that wasn't where I was going. I'd been going to face up to telling her the truth, and risking her disapproval; but I was thankful to be spared and I just let her go on thinking what she liked, and hoping that Tom wouldn't find out. The only thing that really mattered to me was that Neil should have remembered.

He did most of the cooking, though I was quite ready to. He's surprisingly good at it. We had soup, and then an omelette flavoured with herbs out of the garden, and I'd taken him some strawberries as ours are in full swing

just now. We drank wine with the meal; Neil said it was
only Chianti but I thought it was very good. He never
stopped talking. He told me all about when he was young
and poor. His father was a butcher in Liverpool, and he
didn't approve at all of Neil becoming a journalist, which
was how he started his writing. During the war he was
a prisoner in Germany for three years. Being shut up
like that in such awful conditions must have had a lasting effect on him; it's no wonder he's sometimes bad-
tempered. He said he was too cowardly to try and
escape, but I don't believe that. After the war he went
to America, and he's done all sorts of strange things, like
working as a labourer, and in the end going into some
film studios where he was a scene-shifter, then part of
the crowd, and finally a script-writer. He's written the
gossip column for a daily newspaper, and worked in an
hotel, but now he makes so much money from writing
and film-rights that he doesn't have to do anything else.
I could have listened to him all night. Though he made it
sound funny, I felt dreadfully sad to think of his suffering
and loneliness. I couldn't think of what to say. In the end
I said: 'It must have been a very full life,' and he looked
at me strangely.

'I suppose it sounds like that,' he said.

'Hard, of course,' I added hastily, in case he thought I
didn't understand.

'Harder than yours,' he said.

I hadn't meant to draw comparisons.

'Mine's been dull and ordinary,' I told him.

'Whose fault is that? Yours. You could have found
yourself some excitement,' he said.

'I'm not the sort of person exciting things happen to,'

I said. 'Everything just plods along for me. Adventures don't come my way.'

'You've been protected. You're complacent. You've never had to worry about where the next meal's to come from,' Neil said. 'You've always had security.'

Materially, it was true; but only materially. However, because of it I was dull.

'Maybe that's why you're so blastedly meek,' he went on.

'I'm not,' I protested.

'You are. You sit there bashing away at the typewriter, turning the other cheek as hard as you can, while I hurl insults at you and swear in a manner that must revolt your maidenly soul.'

He was mocking me again. 'It wouldn't help if I swore back,' I said hesitatingly.

'How do you know? You haven't tried,' Neil said. 'It might be enormous fun. But your method has its effect. In the end you make me feel a terrible cad.'

He had stopped jeering, and I said with more confidence: 'I don't think you always mean to be as cross as you sound.'

'No, I don't,' he said at once. 'I warned you I'd got a filthy temper. You'd do better to see me no more.'

'You told me your bark was worse than your bite,' I said, with more courage. 'Anyway, it's a business arrangement and I'm paid for putting up with you.'

He laughed. 'So it's worth it, you think?' he said.

I could feel myself turning red. 'Yes,' I said. 'Well worth it.'

He looked at me, smiling, and I felt that he knew exactly what I was thinking, but he didn't tease me this time, or hurry to reply. All the tension and lines of anger had gone from his face, and for a moment he looked almost gentle. This was how he must have been before the bitter, cynical mask he had acquired made him look hard. I wanted to make him keep this mood of relaxation, but I could not think of how to prolong it. He didn't get cross again, though, even when he stopped smiling. Instead, he put a record on and lighted a cigarette, and we sat in peace, listening to Chopin. Neil sprawled in one of the big chairs, and I sat on the sofa. He didn't look at me, but just lay back, staring at the ceiling, in a contented sort of way, and though the usual brandy was beside him he hardly bothered to drink it. I began to wonder whether he would drink so much if he wasn't always alone; so much solitude can't be good for a person. I couldn't accept that Neil, like a hermit, had been designed for isolation. Neil needed sympathetic company, where his rages would not be taken too much to heart and where his work would be respected; it would not, surely, be impossible for him to be happy. Through the length of the record, and all its second side, I speculated, watching him cross the room to turn it over and then go back to his chair. He never looked at me at all.

When the record was over he took a great swig of his forgotten brandy, and then it was that I said he ought to give a bottle to the fête. He looked quite startled when I spoke.

'Oh – do you think so?' he said. I made the remark about the Fabric Fund benefiting more than him, and he replied about the relative values. We sat in silence then, and as he seemed unwilling to talk any more I got up to leave.

'Will you be safe walking home alone, if I don't escort you?' he asked, and now he wore his mocking look again.

'Of course,' I said, knowing he hadn't the slightest intention of coming with me. Anyway, I was not anxious for anyone to see us together, especially as Mother thought I was at Combe. I crossed the stile and went over the field. It wasn't ten yet, a very respectable hour, I thought. The light was fading but it wasn't dark. Bats flitted about above me, and there was dew on the grass. I made a detour round the field so that I would approach home from the direction of Combe just in case I met Daisy McBean or some other busybody. As I came round the side of the hill the faint sound of hammering which I had heard earlier grew louder, and I saw that it was being made by Tom, who was banging away at the fence. Before I could go quickly back he looked up and saw me, and there was nothing for me to do but go on and try to hide the true reason for why I was there. I couldn't think what he was doing at that hour of night, banging away; he had a coil of wire on the ground beside him and seemed to be attaching it to the fence with staples.

'Hallo, Tom, what on earth are you doing?' I said brightly.

He straightened himself and came to help me over the fence. Although I was rather agitated I could not avoid reflecting that Neil would let me climb over unaided. Tom was looking very surprised to see me, reasonably enough.

'What are you doing with all that flex?' I asked, rushing on quickly before he could say anything, for I could see now that the wire was a rubber-covered electric one. Tom, though, was looking at the folder of Neil's work which I carried, and realizing where I had been. I felt guilty and confused.

'I was coming to see you, to ask how your mother is,' I said, for he must be wondering why, if I'd been up at the cottage, I was going home by such a roundabout path.

'Rather a late hour to call, Annie,' he said mildly.

'I haven't been round for ages. I've just been collecting some work from Neil and I thought I'd come back by Combe,' I invented.

'Didn't your friend Addington tell you he'd been reading to Mother this afternoon? Browning's poems,' said Tom. 'She enjoyed it.' He bent to his work again and hammered in a staple with quick, accurate strokes.

I was astounded. 'He didn't tell me. We just talked about the book,' I lied again, miserable at the web of petty deceit now tying me in knots.

Tom picked another staple up out of the tin. 'He met Mother the other day when he came down wanting a plumber,' he said. 'They seemed to get on. Anyway, she was pleased when he offered to read to her. Better than old Nurse's efforts, at least. Brainy chap like that, I suppose he reads well.' He banged the staple home; then he closed the tin. 'Anyway, she'll be tucked up now so you won't be able to see her, Annie. Nice of you to think of coming in. I'll finish this job tomorrow. Come along, I'll walk home with you.'

He stacked the coil of wire neatly under the fence and put the tin in his pocket; then, swinging the hammer, he walked beside me across the field, out into the lane and so home. Explanations and excuses trembled on my lips all the way, but I had said quite enough. I had told at least three lies in ten minutes and I could hardly remember what they were. Part of me felt fierce and defiant; I had every right to see Neil, he needed me and Tom did not; as long as this was so I would be available, and, I knew, with a sinking, lost sensation of inevitability, in any capacity.

The lights were on upstairs; Mother and Father had gone early to bed. Because there was still a limit to my disloyalty, I opened the door quickly and went inside leaving no time for Tom to say good night, but as I went upstairs I realized he had not spoken at all during our short journey home, nor made the slightest gesture towards me. I knew that a thing whose value I could not estimate was slipping from me, and rising in its place was something outside all my experience that it was too **late for me to escape.**

8

Neil

IN spite of my determination to remain aloof, here I am becoming involved with other people. I am tangled already with Anna and the Cartwrights; even, more surprisingly, with Mr Gowberry, the vicar, whose visits I am forced to confess that I enjoy, for he is informed and witty as well as earnest.

It was undeniably kind of Cartwright to insist on arranging a method of communication so that I can summon aid to the cottage in an emergency. Although he made the proposal with some lack of graciousness, he lost no time in putting his idea into action and he has already fixed up, with his own hands, a bell device and a simple code of signals – three short rings for urgent aid, three longer ones for 'no hurry but I need help'. He suddenly grew as enthusiastic as a schoolboy while we tested the contrivance, and to some degree I was infected myself, so that I did not begrudge the valuable time spent in experiment. In helping me, Cartwright has no axe to grind; I am forced to admit that he is acting with complete disinterestedness, at the dictates of his conscience. I assured him that I was most unlikely to need succour, and that if I drank less I would appear to better advantage. He could find no answer to this that was consistent with civility, so I saved him from having to reply by obeying Anna's instructions to give him a bottle of brandy for his tombola. I had the feeling that he was reluctant to take it from me, just as I disliked having to accept his kindness. Against both our wills we are obliged to recognize each other.

I wondered if Anna had disclosed to him how she had spent the evening at the cottage; I was sure she would not willingly reveal that she had stayed to supper, although apart from what may have been going on in her imagination it could scarcely have been a more innocent few hours. Indeed, while the Chopin was playing, I had forgotten that I was not alone and was startled when she suddenly spoke. She has a certain timid appeal when she produces the tenacity to make a sustained contribution to conversation; and her stubborn docility in the face of insult and rudeness is not without effect; at least it succeeds, eventually, in making me feel some shame, and I am almost grateful for having any emotion, even that one, evoked, since I thought myself dead long ago to such sensation.

Fenella and her bursts of retaliation never brought me to shame, though they inspired many other moods. Sometimes I think it would be profitable to lead Anna on, as a diversion for myself and an instruction for her: a year ago I would have obeyed the whim, perhaps in a despairing effort to produce some synthetic force in myself, but not now.

The hour when I read to Mrs Cartwright was a peaceful one. She lay listening, some of the time with closed eyes but occasionally looking out of the window at the garden, and for a time turning to watch me with a calm, steady regard. We did not talk. Afterwards, Nurse Thomson forced tea, scones and home-made jam upon me. I was glad of the tea, but could only make a pretence of dealing with a scone. She began to press for details of my illness, but I would not be drawn and successfully parried her questions. It would not surprise me if she suspected cirrhosis of the liver, from the turn her remarks took. Just as I was leaving, the vicar arrived. He declared that he intends to visit me again very soon, and reminded me that the day of the fête is drawing nearer. Since he seems to think I have some sort of reputation as a celebrity, apart from any other I may be now acquiring, I offered to sign autographs if the sale of them would help to swell the funds.

'Indeed yes, my dear fellow. What a splendid idea,' the vicar said.

'Humiliating, if no one wants it,' I added.

'Oh, they will. They've all heard of the film of *The Breakers*, even if they didn't see it, though I'm not saying they wouldn't be more eager to get Brigitte Bardot's signature than yours,' said the vicar. 'In any case, I've learned from my young friends that a system of swopping abounds. One of yours, added together with several others, might equal a Tommy Steele or Cliff Richard.'

I laughed. Mr Gowberry clearly knew his facts. He smiled, his thin neck bending as he wagged his head.

'I must go and see our dear lady now,' he said. 'How is she, Nurse?'

'Brighter, I'm glad to say,' Nurse Thomson answered. 'Mr Addington's been reading to her. Poetry.' There was a wealth of scorn in the tone with which she uttered the last word. 'Not what I'd have chosen, if my advice had been requested. A nice tale to take them out of themselves, that's what sick people need.'

'Poetry can do that, Nurse,' said Mr Gowberry. 'It can open imagination's doors into fresh pastures,' he added dramatically.

'A nice love story, that's what I'd fancy if I was poorly,' Nurse Thomson insisted.

I was unable to picture the stalwart nurse tucked up, the sheet beneath her chin, indisposed.

'Lots of people share your view, Nurse,' said the vicar heartily. 'But I expect your patient enjoyed the poetry.'

'I think she did,' I said. I looked at Mr Gowberry. 'She's very ill.'

'She's had a terrible shock,' the vicar said. 'Poor woman, a tragic business. So sudden.'

'I'll just pop up and make sure that Mrs Cartwright is tidy, all ready to see you, Vicar,' Nurse said, preparing to dart out of the room. 'I won't be two jiffs.' She hastened away, to my relief. A little of her worthy company was enough for me.

'A good soul,' remarked the vicar, and he grinned, leaving me no doubt but that he interpreted accurately how I felt. I had to smile.

'You're enjoying your stay in Westington,' he went on to inform me. 'It's working out differently from what you expected?'

'I appear to be becoming entangled in personal relationships, which was the last thing I wanted to happen,' I said ruefully.

'My dear fellow, you aren't living if you're avoiding them,' said the vicar. 'Contact, conflict, companionship: the stuff of life. But I hope you aren't getting tangled up, as you put it, with Anna?'

'She's only working for me,' I said mildly.

'She hasn't experience of such people as yourself,' said Mr Gowberry. 'Don't take me amiss; it would be a pity if she was upset.'

I began to protest, but unconvincingly, for I knew that Anna's natural balance had already been disturbed; but the responsibility for that lay with her own vulnerability and not in any action of mine.

'She and Cartwright seem well suited,' I said.

'They are,' Mr Gowberry agreed. 'They are indeed.'

As I walked slowly back to the cottage I reflected on the remarkable perception of the vicar; but perhaps it was not so uncanny; perhaps the situation that I feared might develop was inevitable under such circumstances. A few months ago I would have shrugged off the whole thing as no concern of mine; whilst I still felt innocent of blame for it, I realized that I must tread warily in future.

Back at the cottage the plumber was busy repairing the leak. I was glad to learn the job was nearly done, so that I could soon bath again and would no longer have to fetch water for domestic use from the main tap in the garden. The plumber was a tiny man with a ginger moustache. He wore a dirty cloth cap welded irrevocably to his skull. His assistant was a stout youth who never spoke but handed the various tools across in silence, divining in the manner of a surgeon's skilled team of helpers what was required. I watched for some time, sure that some sort of communication must pass between the two, but detected none. I decided that the boy must be a deaf mute, but was proved wrong when he asked for a brush and dustpan in order to clean up the infinitesimal mess that they left behind after their labours.

They departed, the job done, and I tried to settle down to some work, but concentration eluded me and I could not discipline my thoughts. The weight of my solitude began to press upon me and my mind turned to Fenella with nostalgic regret for what might have been. I thought of my afternoon, spent with Mrs Cartwright, and of how pitiful she was, and yet how admirable, alone and not alone; I thought of her son, ungifted but vigorous, with years before him to extend the roots he already had so firmly established here. My own much vaunted freedom suddenly seemed valueless: who grieved for me and for my frailty? Despair hit me.

In this mood there was no remedy other than brandy; that, at least, had not yet lost its power to comfort. I had drunk quite a lot of it when Anna arrived bearing her homework in a parcel before her, and I felt languidly fatalistic. I peered at her hazily: she looked somehow different; there was an air of suppressed defiance about her, and her eyes, not usually a noticeable feature, blazed fiercely, looking larger. When she diagnosed my condition she uttered a sound of mingled dismay and resignation and laid down her parcel of manuscript. Then she came over to me, took the glass that I was holding out of my hand, and put it away well out of my reach.

I caught hold of her hand. Vaguely the words of Mr Gowberry echoed in my head, but I did not listen. Anna at least was real; and she found me important. Her face, looking slightly alarmed, came nearer; she was valiant, and committed.

9

Anna

IN Westington weeks can pass uneventfully, with very little to distinguish the days from each other, and then suddenly everything begins to happen at once with one crisis after another boiling furiously up, leaving no time for the first to be dealt with before the next has arrived. All the time that I have been slowly getting more and more involved with Neil, village activities have continued. The strawberry glut has come, and my back is permanently bent so that I am like a hoop from constant picking. We have had extra help from the village women, who enjoy this source of extra revenue, but we could have done with more. Mother went away to stay with Marjorie while this was going on; she knows how to time her exits. She came back with tales of the twins' exploits at school but nothing much to say about Lal, except that she's plainer than ever and now has to wear glasses to cap all. She is to be allowed to come down for the fête; it will do her good, poor kid, to have a rest from Marjorie and Hugh, who hardly bother to talk to her at all, or if they do they treat her with such impatient patience that you'd think she was a half-wit. Now I'm horrified at myself because in a way I wish she wasn't coming after all. It means I'll have to look after her and keep her happy and I won't have time for Neil; his work will have to wait and I won't be able to escape up to the cottage in the afternoons. But, of course, it will only be for a week-end, and the fête will occupy all Saturday in any case.

Mrs Fanshawe has been round for contributions to the fancy stall. Mother as usual had a host of things ready that she'd bought at other fêtes all over the county where she has to go. She's in great demand as an opener, because of her magisterial fame, and of course she always has to buy things at every stall wherever she goes; anyway this system means she can always produce something on demand, from pin-cushions to matinée coats, and so far nothing has reappeared close enough to its place of origin to be recognized. She doled out handkerchiefs and bath salts and a rather weird tea-cosy which Mrs Fanshawe carried off in high glee. Mrs Gowberry is

doing the cakes this year; I suppose I shall have to make
one for her; what a nuisance it all is.

But in fact last year I enjoyed the fête; I always do in
the end, in spite of all the work and behind-the-scenes
warfare that goes on. Last year it broke the monotony,
and there wasn't anything else in particular that I was
clamouring to do, whereas now I grudge every moment
that keeps me away from the book, or stops me going to
see Neil. It was after last year's fête that Tom and I got
engaged: somehow it all seems much longer ago than
that. At the time I felt happy; it meant there would be
an end to my imprisonment as dutiful daughter of the
house, and besides, I was fond of Tom and used to him,
and I was glad. We'd been happy, packing up the tombola drum and the bottles that were left over, making
silly jokes and laughing. Now everything is different; it's
all over, and I dread to meet him, but I must tell him
so. It's dishonest to drift on like this. I know now that
even if Neil hits me over the head the next time I go up
there he'll still matter more to me than anyone else. I
suppose this is being in love: it isn't very comfortable;
I feel half-afraid, anxious, and yet wildly elated all at
the same time. I'm like a motor-car that's suddenly got
two extra cylinders to fire on; everything's happening at
a much faster rate than before, and I've lost control of
the road.

That evening, before I went up to the cottage, I'd
made up my mind: I knew that I must break it off with
Tom so that I was free. If Neil knew that had happened
there would be a difference at once; he was always
jibing and jeering at Tom and mocking about what a
dull life we'd have; well, he won't be able to do that

any more. And though I haven't got any brains I've learnt a lot from Neil already and he can soon teach me more. I think he enjoys it when we talk; I argue sometimes when he's in a good humour, and he doesn't seem to mind now. He'll still not agree that people don't always have an ulterior motive for what they do: he says nothing is ever done disinterestedly, that people are always on the look-out for future benefits as a result of what they do, even if they don't know it themselves. I don't believe that; I can't accept that everyone is like the characters in his book moving like a lot of chessmen laying traps or insurances, but perhaps virtue is dull and therefore doesn't make literature.

In the end, that evening, it wasn't necessary to tell Neil anything. He was sitting on the sofa with the brandy bottle beside him and a glass as usual in his hand. He looked ill, and his eyes had an odd, strained expression in them that wasn't only alcohol. He's even thinner than he was when first he came here. He looked rather wuzzily at me, as though he couldn't see me very clearly, but I didn't feel disapproving or alarmed. I simply took his glass away. He didn't try to stop me, but he caught hold of my hand. His fingers are so thin that you can feel their bones distinctly. I felt very calm, all the time.

But the next day he had disappeared. In the morning, directly after breakfast, I hurried up the hill to see how he was, and he had gone. The cottage was locked and deserted, and there was no clue as to where he had vanished to, only a note to the milkman saying not to come till further notice. In the middle of my agitation I found myself being amazed at Neil even thinking of this. When he came here he hadn't a clue about minor domestic matters and cared less. But there wasn't a message for me. To begin with, I couldn't get in as naturally I hadn't brought a key, and when I got home I had to help Father in the office, so that it was afternoon before I could get back again and let myself in.

There was chaos inside: his bed was in a tumble and his clothes were falling out of a drawer. All morning I'd been panicking in case he had gone for good, in spite of the note to the milkman, stricken with remorse or something, but at least that didn't seem likely. I decided not to be hurt because he'd left no message; he'd been alone so long that he didn't think of other people worrying. I thought his publisher might have suddenly sent for him, or the film people; but as there was no way of solving the mystery I set about clearing up the mess. It took some time, as it seemed a good chance for giving the place a thorough going over. When I went into the kitchen to fetch the sweeper I noticed a new electric switch hanging from a heavy cable near the back door; it was a bell-push. I pressed it two or three times but there was no sound, so if Neil was suddenly becoming mechanical and fitting himself up with a back-door bell he certainly hadn't finished the job successfully. It seemed a funny thing for him to have done, but I stopped puzzling about it and went off to get on with the cleaning, which still left my mind unoccupied and able to go on speculating about the more urgent problem of when Neil would be back.

About ten minutes later Tom came bursting into the cottage. He looked astonished at seeing me, but he wasn't more surprised than I was to see him.

'Where's Addington?' he demanded, looking round as

if Neil might be hiding under the table. 'What's wrong?'

'There's nothing wrong that I know of,' I said. I'd been polishing the tiles in front of the fireplace, and now I got up slowly to face Tom.

'But the bell rang,' Tom said. 'I thought perhaps he'd had another turn and was too ill to get away.'

'What bell? What turn? I don't know what you're talking about, Tom,' I said.

'The bell to Combe. He had a funny turn when he was down the other day, so I fixed him up a bell to ring in case he got another,' Tom said impatiently.

'So that's what it is,' I said. 'I rang it. I didn't know. I thought it was some sort of back-door bell.' I remembered seeing Tom twining the electric cable round the fence and securing it with staples: so that was what he had been doing. 'I'm sorry, Tom, dragging you up here for nothing.'

'Well, perhaps it's as well that I've come,' Tom said grimly. 'I wanted to talk to you anyway.'

I felt a sinking sensation in my stomach; it had to come, but now that the moment had arrived I wanted to postpone it. I harked back to an earlier remark of Tom's.

'Did you know Neil was going away?' I asked.

'He came down early this morning to say he'd got to go to London. Business, and some medical check he has to have sometimes,' Tom said shortly. 'He used the phone to get a taxi. He looked pretty ghastly, so I thought he might have changed his mind about going.'

'I see.' It seemed a very sudden decision, made overnight, unless the postman had brought a letter that had caused him to hurry away.

'Anna,' Tom said now, gravely, 'I don't want to make

a fuss about trifles, but it isn't right for you to be here cleaning up after Addington at all hours of the clock. Do his typing, if you feel you must; anyway, you can't let him down half-way through the job, but he must get someone in from the village to do his cleaning. You've got quite enough to do already, and besides it isn't appropriate.'

'I don't do much,' I said weakly. 'I'm only doing this because I came up to fetch some typing and found he'd gone and left a shambles behind. I like the cottage, Tom; I don't want it to get into a mess. And he doesn't like strangers.'

'I know. But you were once a stranger, too,' Tom said. 'Maggie Potter would come up, and he'd soon get used to her.'

'But I like doing it,' I insisted.

Tom hesitated. Then he said: 'Anna, I'm sorry, but I don't like you doing it and I must insist that you stop. I'm not being stuffy. I accept that you must continue with the clerical work, but housekeeping is another thing and I'm surprised that Addington agrees to it.'

'He hardly notices,' I said. 'He does some himself, after all. I only do bits when he's writing.'

'Well, please stop,' Tom said heavily. 'I ask you to, Anna.'

I took a deep breath.

'And what if I refuse?' I demanded.

Tom looked at me then; indeed, his eyes had never left my face since he entered the room. I found that I could not meet his gaze. I felt bitterly ashamed of what I was doing, but I had to go on.

'Do you refuse, Anna?' he asked.

'Yes, I do,' I said. I swallowed. 'Tom, I can't marry you now.'

It was done. The words were uttered.

At first Tom said nothing, but he turned away. Then he swung round and faced me again.

'Because of Addington?' It was more a statement than a question, but I answered it.

'Yes. Because of Neil,' I said.

There was a silence. Several times Tom seemed about to say something, but he changed his mind and stayed silent. At last he spoke.

'He'll never marry you, Anna,' he said.

'In time he might decide to,' I said defiantly.

'I can think of at least three reasons why he won't, Anna, and none of them is a reflection on you,' Tom said. 'For one thing, he's very ill.'

'I know. But he'd get better much more quickly if he had someone to look after him,' I declared.

'Maybe. But he's a rolling stone, my dear. Here today, next week in Timbuctoo. You didn't even know he was going away today, he didn't take the trouble to leave you a note, did he?'

It was true.

'You only knew because he wanted to use your phone,' I said, defending my own position. 'And he may have wanted to be sure your mother wouldn't expect him to come and read to her.'

Although this side of Neil's character was incomprehensible to me, for it was so unlike the rest of him, it was useful now as an illustration of his thoughtful nature.

'You think in time he'll want to marry you, although

at present he bothers more about my mother's feelings than yours?' Tom asked.

I didn't really think that Neil ever would, but I hoped, and on hope one can exist indefinitely.

'Your mother's ill,' I snapped. 'I'm not.'

'I'm not so sure, my dear,' Tom said. He looked so sad suddenly that an enormous lump came into my throat, but I had to continue.

'I love him, anyway,' I declared loudly.

It sounded theatrical, said like that; I felt it was the most important statement I had ever made in my life.

'Then there's nothing else that I can say,' Tom said. He looked suddenly stricken and old. He walked away across the room, with his back to me, and stared out of the window. I just stood and watched him, and presently he turned and came back to me. He put his hands gently on my arms, holding me.

'Anna, believe me, I've met men like Addington before and you haven't. He has many merits, I'm sure, but he has no intention of marrying you or anyone else, whatever he may have led you to believe. He's here in the village for just a short time, to convalesce and to write his book. It's an interlude to him, and you're a temporary asset. When he leaves he'll forget you. He's got no room in his life for permanent ties and responsibility. You're only going to be badly hurt.'

'I can't help that. It's a risk I must accept,' I said.

Tom dropped his hands and moved away again. He seemed lost and uncertain; I had never seen him indecisive before. I could hear my heart banging away loudly. Part of me longed to put the clock back twenty-four hours so that I could return to safety, but part of

me fumed with impatience to be finished with this inter-
view and have the way ahead clear.

'Very well, Annie,' Tom said at last. 'I accept what
you've told me, and as far as we are both concerned,
neither of us is bound in any way to the other. But I
beg you to keep it just to ourselves – and Addington,
if he doesn't already know your views. Till you've had
longer to make sure.'

I was going to protest, but before I could do so he
went on.

'There are several reasons, Annie, why I ask you not
to act hastily. The most important one is because I am
afraid for you and want you to be quite sure before you
create a situation which will affect not only you, but your
whole family, and all the village too. The next reason
is because I think you are chasing a rainbow as far as
Addington is concerned, and if that proves to be so, even
if you never go back to wanting to marry me, I want to
be in a position to help you; there's no haste needed in
making public a broken engagement when there's no
wedding to be cancelled. The other reason is purely
selfish: quite honestly I've as much on my plate now as
I can cope with without having to return wedding presents and accept still more condolences from the county.'

'Oh, Tom!' I was appalled to discover that I had given
no thought to practical considerations. I was so pre-
occupied with my own desires that I had not seen beyond
them, apart from the necessity to stop pretending to Tom.
I had not realized the enormity of the blow I was aiming
at him, but now the full meaning of his words began to
sink in.

'You can't still want to marry me, after what I've said?'
I asked him.

'I don't want to marry you unless that's what you want
too,' he said. 'But you did. In fact only a week ago you
even seemed eager. We've known each other all our lives,
and I've loved you for so many years that I can't really
believe a stranger can separate us for long. If you discover you've made a mistake, Annie, don't be too proud
to admit it.'

I couldn't answer him. We stood looking at one another
in silence; I had never seen Tom like this before, and I
had not known that it was in my power to hurt him so
much.

He said: 'You agree, Anna, to say nothing?'

I nodded.

He kissed me then, quickly and gently, on the lips.
His mouth was soft and tender. I just stood there, incapable of movement, and watched him leave. When he
had gone I moved to the window so that I could see him
cross the field. He never once turned to look back, but
as he walked away over the grass he no longer held himself with his usual erect, almost military carriage; now
he moved slowly, and was stooped, as if old and defeated.

I flung myself on to the sofa and burst into tears.

10

Neil

MUCH has changed since I first came to Westington over a month ago. The lilacs have faded, but roses bloom on cottage walls, and more blaze about the gardens. Everywhere, the light fresh green of early summer foliage has given way to a deeper colour. I was glad to be back, and not only because of the grim reason for my absence; the cottage, I felt fancifully, welcomed me home.

Anna had cleaned up: all was as neat as on the day of my first arrival, and a pile of freshly typed manuscript waited for me on the table. My memory of what had happened during the hours immediately before my departure was hazy; I recalled Anna removing the brandy glass from my hand, and her look of desperate courage, in face of which my own physical humiliation had been complete. Morning had brought its usual greeting of panic, remorse and nausea; I had forgotten Anna in the mounting terror that made me realize what must happen.

During the time I spent in London, Westington seemed remote, a dream place fading farther into unreality until I was convinced that I would never return there; then a curious determination to fulfil my undertaking of opening that ridiculous fête for Gowberry obsessed me; that, together with the compulsion of my work, drew me on, so that here I was, back again and just in time to carry out my obligation.

It was an effort, meanwhile, to start work: I skimmed through the pages that Anna had left for me and made a few adjustments; then I got out my notes, but after half an hour I had achieved very little more. I yielded to the temptation of alternative occupation and decided to go down to the village. I would announce my return to Mrs Potter and ask her to tell the milkman and the baker that their services were once more required.

The day was warm, with the sun high in the sky and only a few wispy clouds to be seen. A drowsy dog lay in the road, dozing near the pond, and outside the village hall a small group of people waited to catch the afternoon bus into Chawton. Among them I discerned Mrs Potter, resplendent and unmistakable in her purple coat and hat. I had forgotten that it was Westington's early closing day.

This was a setback. I had been looking forward, I realized, to a conversation with Mrs Potter and perhaps also with some of her juvenile customers, and now my purpose was foiled. The Grapes was closed, so that I could not pursue diversion there. There was nothing left for me now but to return to the cottage and make a disciplined effort to do some work. I turned about and trudged up the lane, bad-tempered and depressed because thwarted. A car came towards me from Chawton, its tyres churning the dust of the dry road; it slowed to take the bend, and the driver, recognizing me, inclined her head in gracious acknowledgement; it was Mrs Harris, homeward bound, I assumed, after a session on the Bench. I nodded back, with equal regality, and wondered idly if she felt a smug glow of virtue in having made this gesture towards one of whom she thoroughly disapproved. She would never descend low enough to ignore me, but to

one with her inflexibly Establishment outlook I was un-
mistakably *non persona grata.*

It occurred to me that I could gain a brief reprieve
for myself and put off the moment of the return to work
if I went round by Combe Farm and paid a call on Mrs
Cartwright, but after looking at my watch I realized that
I would coincide with tea-time, and I had not the forti-
tude to cope with Nurse Thomson's scones. Tomorrow, I
resolved, I would gather my forces and at a less inhibit-
ing hour I would walk down there and find out how my
fellow-traveller was faring.

My meandering thoughts were interrupted by a sudden
call from behind me.

'Mr Addington, Mr Addington! Cooee–ee!'

I turned round, and saw that it was Mrs Gowberry
who was hailing me. She bustled up the road towards
me, clutching a large, shabby basket in one hand. She
is a plump person, shaped rather like a cottage loaf, with
pepper-and-salt hair springing untidily round her head in
wiry corkscrews, and much given to wearing little shawls
or stoles; on this occasion a bright mustard-coloured one
was draped round her shoulders, in spite of the warm
weather. It was slipping as she hurried along, and she
tugged it back into place with a movement that was now
a habit.

I found myself changing direction so that I walked to
meet her and relieved her of the basket that she carried.

'Oh, thank you, thank you,' she puffed. 'I'm on my way
to the church to clean the brass. Friday is my day,
usually, but this week I'll be too busy preparing for the
fête so I'm just popping along now. How nice to see you
back again. When did you return?'

'This morning,' I told her, falling into step beside her. She pattered along, two strides to my one, her feet in vivid blue raffia sandals.

'We've missed you. Fred went up to the cottage several times to see if you'd come back,' she said. I was not sure if I imagined the note of reproof in her voice, but I felt remorse at the thought of the unfortunate vicar panting up the hill pushing his bicycle only to find that his errant sheep was still absent. There was always, I knew, an element of uncertainty also about his journey down, coasting along with the wind of his passage blowing his wispy hair on end, for his machine was notable more for its museum vintage than for its efficiency.

'I should have written to the vicar,' I said, vaguely apologetic.

'You went so suddenly,' she said. 'Tom told us you'd had to go. We were worried in case you were kept away till after the fête, but Fred said you'd be here.'

'I nearly wasn't,' I told her. 'I almost failed to make it.'

She looked at me penetratingly, and I wondered how much she knew of what the vicar had deduced. By now we had reached the lych gate of the church, and I unlatched it, pausing to let her pass through before following her.

'Well, I'm glad you managed,' was all she said, and then, with an approving glance about her at the pale, freshly scythed grass of the churchyard: 'McBean has finished the mowing, I see. How tidy it looks.' I wondered what difference it made to the bundles of bones rotting here whether the grass above was long or short, whether indeed many of them were even remembered. Bright little offerings of flowers were dotted about, many

wilting, among the tombstones, and I speculated about
how many of these were manifestations of affection or
merely the tributes of duty.

'Your parents are living?' Mrs Gowberry inquired.

'My father died three years ago,' I told her. 'I hadn't
seen him for ten years.' We went into the little church,
cool and smelling faintly damp and mossy. She knelt,
briefly and unostentatiously, for a few seconds, and I
felt strangely unembarrassed; it never occurred to me to
leave her there alone, and soon I found myself holding
a large cloth which had once been part of the vicar's
winter vest and industriously rubbing Brasso on to an
altar vase. Gradually I discovered that I was revealing
to Mrs Gowberry the unedifying history of my early life.
'My mother left my father when I was quite a small kid,'
I said. 'She was a gentle, artistic creature as I remember
her, and he was just a hulk of flesh – he was a butcher,
and as red, ugly and savage as his own raw meat. Mother
ran away with a violinist from the orchestra of a third-
rate touring opera company. Eventually they went to
Canada and she died there when I was eleven. She'd
always planned to send for me when she could scrape up
the fare. But in any case my father would never have let
me go – not because he had any affection for me, he
hadn't, but to spite her. I'd have escaped in time – I did,
of course, but it was too late by then.'

'Poor man.' Mrs Gowberry patted my hand as I laid
down the vase, now shining, and picked up a candlestick.
'What a sad story. Still, you must comfort yourself by
remembering how proud your mother would have been
of your success.'

'Of course, you think she knows about it?' I remarked, mocking her.

'Aware, certainly. Don't you?' she countered.

'I do not,' I replied. 'She had a drab and wretched life. In my sentimental moments, which aren't many, I like to imagine that she had some happiness with her violinist, but in fact I know they lived in utter poverty and were probably as miserable as they were poor. Meanwhile my brutish father prospered, and could at least have provided her with material security. I'm glad now that she died before she grew old; to me she's burnt out, like a spent match — pfff!' I snapped my fingers, blackened now with tarnish from the brass. I felt that I was behaving melodramatically, but Mrs Gowberry remained undisturbed. She carried the pair of shining vases back to the altar and replaced them, one at either side.

'They look nice,' she said, with truth. 'I like to see visible proof of the benefits of my labours, don't you?' Without waiting for a reply she went on: 'You still remember your mother. Don't you think that that is immortality of a sort?'

'Only for as long as I am alive. She'll be forgotten after that,' I said.

'There's a more positive way for you, even with your rationalist outlook, to think,' Mrs Gowberry said. She stopped rubbing the ornate book-rest that she held, in order to address me with extra conviction. 'As long as your work survives, so will the earthly memory of your mother.'

Subconsciously, I suppose, I had already admitted this. However, in the space of an afternoon, even though aided by the atmosphere of the church, in itself a testament to faith, Mrs Gowberry was not able to convert me to belief in a celestial hereafter. In fact, oblivion seemed to me to be an eminently desirable condition, comparable with the release of dreamless sleep. I hoped, of course, that my work would endure through at least some succeeding generations, if the politicians allowed any to exist, as social documents which would provoke, stimulate and disturb, but such hopes as these were vain, I was sure.

'Well, now, you must come back to the rectory for tea,' said Mrs Gowberry when we had finished our labours, and besides the dazzling display of vases and candlesticks all the commemorative tablets and plaques on the walls had been rendered brilliant again. When I demurred she insisted: 'Nonsense. Having press-ganged you into helping me, and preached at you for half an hour, you must let me make some amends.'

I laughed. Even though I remained sceptical at least I had learned that the little church, with its ancient oak pews and small side chapel kept for the children's services, was a peaceful refuge.

'I've enjoyed myself,' I confessed. 'I like an argument. But thank you, I'd like tea too.'

'A discussion, rather,' Mrs Gowberry told me in reproof, smiling. Her wild hair was even more unruly now, and her face was flushed with exertion as well as its network of tiny broken veins which lent it a permanent rosy colour.

We returned through the village together, past the pond where now the road was occupied by a group of children fresh from school, playing hopscotch. The rectory was a huge Victorian house with miles of draughty passages, and the childless Gowberrys must have felt lost, often, in its vast emptiness.

'The clergy always used to produce large families,' Mrs Gowberry told me as we went into the kitchen, an enormous high-ceilinged room reminiscent of a baronial hall. 'This must have been a splendid house in those days, when maids abounded and stipends were adequate.'

I wondered how much she minded being childless; whether her parish toils, her scarves and stoles, and the vicar's welfare offered enough scope for sublimation.

'Fred's out,' Mrs Gowberry told me as she put the kettle on. 'He'll be sorry to miss you. He's round at Mrs Watts's – she hasn't been too well lately and the boys – her evacuated children, she calls them, and of course they're family men now – are a bit anxious about her. I expect he'll have a cup of tea with her.'

We had ours in the garden under the shade of a big old tree – a cedar, my hostess told me, assuming correctly my ignorance. It was peaceful. I wondered why one ever sought any other kind of life than this, and yet I knew that my pleasure in it could only be short-lived; in health, such quietness would swiftly drive me mad with impatience and boredom. After tea I made the excuse of work and hurried off, retreating from my thoughts, up the hill.

II

Anna

I NEVER knew the days could pass so slowly. Since Neil
vanished I seem to have died a thousand times. At first I
tried not to think about him, but when I was typing out
his book it was as if I could hear his voice dictating, with
all the time a suspicion of mockery in it. All day, whatever I'm doing, he's there in my mind; but chiefly there's
the hurt, so, so big, because he went like that without a
word. Every day I expected a letter to arrive, explaining;
every day when I took the letters out of the box and
quickly sorted them my heart beat faster, hopefully, and
then gave a despairing lurch of disappointment so that I
was almost in tears. Such a little act from him, a few lines
quickly scrawled, and such a lot it would have meant to
me to know he'd thought about me even for five minutes.

But he never wrote. After a week I tried to stop hoping, but with small success. I invented a dozen excuses
from a broken wrist to a stolen mailbag to account for
why no letter came, but all the time the real reason, that
he'd forgotten me, was hiding in the shadows for me to
recognize.

But now he's back. Suddenly the misery of all this time
doesn't matter any more, and I'm busy pretending to
myself and everyone else that I don't mind having discovered quite by chance that he's returned. It was a
complete fluke that I found out. I'd gone up to the rectory
to fetch some jam and home-made sweets Mrs Gowberry
had promised for my stall – it's easier, I find, to get

everything together myself in plenty of time and not
depend on the kind donors to deliver it on the spot at
the last moment, one knows where one is then. Mrs
Gowberry's fudge is delicious and is pounced on at once,
and even Mother likes her marrow jam. I don't know
what she puts into it that gives it such a kick, mine's always so nondescript, just like me in fact. When I arrived,
Mrs Gowberry was getting supper ready for herself and
the vicar – macaroni cheese, rather stodgy, I privately
thought, in such hot weather. She hadn't washed up the
tea things, in fact she was in a good deal of a muddle, as
she often is, and I helped her to sort herself out as otherwise I'd never have got my jam and stuff. She'd left a pile
of filthy old rags and a tin of Brasso on the draining-
board, all among the crockery, and I made some remark
about it – I think she's a perfect saint doing all that
polishing in the church, there's such a lot of it, dozens of
memorial plates stuck on the wall as well as all the altar
equipment. It must be a hideous bind every week. She
said she'd had a helper this time, and when I asked who,
told me it was Neil.

I couldn't have been more surprised if she'd told me it
was the Queen herself – less, in fact. Not only because
the news meant that Neil was back, but of all the most
unlikely occupations for him, this one was worthy of
top place. Even his reading to Mrs Cartwright is easier
to understand for at least books are his subject.

'We had a long talk,' Mrs Gowberry told me. 'Poor
man, he's had such a sad life, but I think he's becoming
more content now.'

She wouldn't say any more, and of course she'd never
reveal a word anyone said to her in confidence, but she

did tell me he'd had tea with her. I wondered which of the cups Neil had used. There were dregs of sugar undissolved in one, and I decided that was his; he was greedy about sugar, and I knew Mrs Gowberry wouldn't be so wasteful. It made me feel odd, holding the cup before I washed it up and thinking that Neil had drunk from it not long before. It must have been an unusual experience for him too, as he doesn't go in for tea very much though he knows I prop myself up with it whenever I get the chance. Pounds of coffee for Neil, and brandy, of course; beer too, but not much tea.

I left the rectory at last, nearly forgetting the jam in my stupid state. My one desire was to go rushing up the hill to the cottage to see him, but there was so much to do at home that I hadn't a chance of getting away till after supper, and then I was suddenly afraid. If I went, he might be angry; or worse, he might tease me. I kept changing my mind about what was best, until it was so late that I couldn't go. Instead, I went to bed, where at least I could be alone and not feel Father peering into my conscience or Mother emanating despair of me.

It was a fine night, and I leaned out of my window looking at the stars and the little moon and thinking foolishly that Neil might be gazing at them too. I wondered what he was doing. He might be working, but I was afraid that if I'd been able to see into the cottage I'd have discovered him to be drinking instead. Slowly a wild excitement at the prospect of seeing him again, tomorrow for sure, surged inside me. It helped to dispel the agonizing hurt; I would not let it rise within me but stifled it, concentrating on what was good, on the hope that he wouldn't get angry with me but be nice, and

not make fun of me. Although I'd a million things to do
the next day I'd go up somehow; I'd manage it before
meeting Lalage at Chawton station. I wished now that
she wasn't coming for the week-end, and then was
ashamed of myself because I knew it meant so much to
her, and because really I want her, I'm so fond of her.
These days I don't seem to know myself at all; I hardly
seem to sleep, and I'm cross and edgy and bad-tempered;
I've behaved atrociously to Tom, and yet I scarcely
bother to give him half a thought much less indulge in
guilty remorse. In fact I haven't spoken to him since that
day at the cottage after Neil had gone. Once or twice
I've seen him in the distance and dodged him; I cut
church on Sunday, daring Mother's wrath by saying I'd
got a headache, which was true, so I didn't see him then.
On Saturday we'll have to meet, of course, at the fête,
and go on in front of the village as if nothing had happened. I suppose it's reasonable of Tom to ask me to
do that; anyway I dread coping with all the undoing
that must be done, too. Sometimes I wonder where all
this will end; I seem to have no control at all over myself
or over events.

That night I went round to the Fanshawes to see if
Betty would let Lally have some rides over the week-
end. All the ponies are out in their paddock getting
steadily fatter, and I'm sure they'll be pleased to have
some of them exercised; Lal is big enough to manage
Joey well now. While I was there Dr Fanshawe came in.

'Ha, Anna!' he said heartily, like he always does. If
you've got 'flu his cheery manner makes you feel better
at once, but at this particular moment his exuberance
made me feel like hitting him, I'm afraid. 'I've just seen

your young man,' he added. For an insane moment I thought he meant Neil, until of course I realized he'd been to see Mrs Cartwright; he goes to Combe about twice a week. 'Looking rather down in the dumps, your Tom,' he went on. 'He's got a lot on his plate, poor fellow. You ought to name the day, Anna, and go and help him.'

I couldn't think how to reply.

'Tom says it wouldn't be fair on his mother,' I said weakly, blaming Tom, for though in fact he had said this, none of the damage was his fault.

'So he told me,' nodded Dr Fanshawe. I thought, good grief, he's been nagging at Tom and got nowhere, and now he's trying to get at me. 'I don't agree. Told him so. Think she'd be glad, now. She's as well as she'll ever be, I'm afraid; may go on like this for months or even years. You're neither of you getting any younger. Time you both started a family – might buck her up too.'

I writhed. Luckily Betty came to my rescue; she's a tactful creature.

'I expect Tom and Anna know what they're doing, Bill,' she said. 'You mustn't interfere. Lalage is coming for the week-end and Pam's going to take her out with the ponies tomorrow afternoon.'

'Ah, good, splendid, I like Lalage,' said Dr Fanshawe. 'Nice kid. Odd man out at home, isn't she?'

There he went, always bang on the nail; he doesn't miss a trick. Once he'd got off the subject of Tom and me I didn't object so much to his powers of accurate intuition, so I threw myself enthusiastically into discussing Lalage. Luckily the telephone summoned him away before the subject was exhausted. I thought how difficult it must be to be married to a doctor: they never have a

minute's peace free from fear of interruption, and have
to turn out in the night goodness knows how often. Still,
Betty seems to like it. She's so pretty and gay, and all
the children are pleasant and well-mannered; she's certainly made a success of her life and it can't have been
easy.

Father's been rather quiet lately. He's still reading six
thrillers a week, the girl in the library is getting quite
fed up with him since she can't keep pace with his rate
of consumption, and he's always demanding the newest
ones long before they've even been heard of in Chawton; but I've caught him looking at me sometimes when
I've been going into a trance instead of concentrating on
the pricking out or whatever I'm meant to be doing. He
hasn't said anything, though. Mother's been out a lot,
thank goodness, visiting prisons without bars, and so on.
She'll be well to the fore on Saturday, of course, busy
with her Lady Bountiful act as queen of the village.

Before I left the Fanshawes I went down to the field
with Pam to look at the ponies. She's a nice child, older
than Lal but not a bit condescending and seems pleased
to have the prospect of company over her half-term holi-
day. She's as tall as I am now, and very pretty with her
long, fair hair and that little peppering of freckles on her
nose. She'll be lovely when she has her plaits off and
appears as a grown-up. I feel envious of her because of
her appearance and her poise. How much easier life will
be for her than for poor Lal, for instance, with her spectacles and her flat feet.

In a week's time the fête will be a thing of the past,
Lal will be back at school, and Richard will have come on
leave, we heard from him last Monday. What else, I

wonder, will have happened? Will Neil have asked me to
supper again? At least he'll want me to finish his typing,
if nothing more. I'll go up and see him tomorrow afternoon while Lal is riding with Pam. After all, he'll be
expecting me: he'll know that village gossip will have
spread the news of his return.

12

Neil

WHAT a situation! That poor girl Anna! Goodness
knows, I may be a graceless, scrounging no-good, but at
least where she is concerned, apart from a few seconds'
momentary, but only mental, lapse, I thought I'd played
fair, and that she knew the limits of my aims and
capabilities.

She came up to the cottage the day after my return. It
was early afternoon, and the air was hot and oppressive,
as if a storm threatened. Anna was overheated, and not
looking her best when she appeared at the stile. I had
been dozing after a poor night, spread out in a deck-
chair under the shade of a tree, and although I wanted
her to take away last night's quota of work to type for
me, I resented the interruption; however, I pulled myself
together and made an effort to seem welcoming as she
approached my refuge. She brought her customary offering; Anna never arrives at the cottage empty-handed, and
today it was eggs and raspberries.

'Ah, there you are, Anna,' I said bracingly, not getting
up.

The poor creature blushed from the top of her boat-necked gingham dress to the roots of her untidy brown hair. She looked nervous, and was clutching the basket she carried as desperately as if it contained the Crown Jewels, tightly with both hands. Foreboding filled me.

'I heard you were back,' she said, accusingly.

It had never occurred to me to inform her of my movements.

'Yes,' I said, on the defensive, realizing too late that some courtesy was due to her, for she had restored order to the chaos that I had left behind and she had efficiently completed the work I had left for her. However, I knew that it thrilled her to be, however remotely, connected with the world of art, and I had brought an excitement and an increase in *tempo* into her monotonous existence; she should be grateful and undemanding. I had not considered that these benefits might have less estimable side effects.

'You never said you were going away,' she mumbled, the slight defiance she had at first displayed now dwindling.

'I didn't know myself till the last minute,' I replied with truth. I decided to apply a balm. 'I left rather a mess, I'm afraid. Thanks for coping. You shouldn't have bothered.' The last remark was a mere formality, for I knew that her feeling for the little cottage was a sincere one and she hated to see the place in disorder.

'It was all right. Did you find your clean shirts? The laundry came, but I couldn't find much to send.'

I nodded. As Anna had always dealt with this chore I was scarcely aware of the laundry's existence but merely reimbursed her for its cost. I felt guilty; her efficient organization was something I took for granted, and perhaps I presumed too much, but it was the way I ran my life. She was not meeting my eyes squarely, and a muscle twitched in her cheek. I realized that beneath her commonplace exterior turmoil raged.

'I'm sorry I didn't let you know when I'd be back,' I said.

'It's all right,' she said again. 'Why should you?' Her attempt at indifference intensified my discomfort. I tried to change the subject.

'How's everything?' I asked. 'As busy as ever in the garden?'

She nodded.

'We're in the middle of the soft-fruit season,' she said. 'There's a lot of picking to be done. We've got my niece Lalage staying, too, for the fête. She's out riding now with Pam Fanshawe.'

'Oh.' I could think of no apt comment, so to avoid a weighty silence I asked: 'How's the boy friend?'

She looked away at once and shifted the basket which she still held from one hand to the other. Her bare, sunburnt arms were scratched, presumably from her horticultural activities, and her strong hands were hard and calloused, as I knew. It was uncomfortable, conversing thus, looking up at her and squinting at the sun, so that at last I got slowly to my feet and she turned then to face me.

'I haven't seen him,' she replied, and took a deep breath. Then, her words tumbling out, she went on: 'It's all off between us, Neil, but it's a secret. Tom doesn't want to cope with all the fuss of a broken engagement just now, but it's over.'

I was dumbfounded, and yet, in a way, not surprised, for there was something about her general demeanour that had led me to anticipate portentous tidings.

'Whose idea was this?' I asked, for something must be said.

She turned away and began drawing patterns on the grass with her schoolgirl's sandal.

'Mine,' she said. 'I broke it off.'

'But why, Anna?' I asked, although with a sinking heart I was sure I knew. 'You were so well suited, what a pity.' And indeed, amazingly, I felt that a sad thing had happened.

'You wouldn't have said that a month ago,' she said, and she was right. 'You'd have applauded.' Anna spoke with astonishing truculence. 'You thought our future stretched out like a barren desert before us,' she continued dramatically.

'Cartwright's a very sound fellow,' I said. 'I know him better now. I think you're making a mistake, Anna.'

She became calm. 'I can't possibly marry him now,' she said. 'You, of all people, should understand that. It would be utterly dishonest, and anyway I couldn't do it.'

'You mean you're not in love with him? But I don't suppose you ever were,' I said. 'That didn't stop you from embarking on all this. Heaps of people marry for practical considerations and they have quite as much chance of happiness as anyone else; more, possibly, since they expect less.'

'I've always been fond of Tom, and I'm too fond of him to do this,' Anna said in a low voice. 'I respect him.'

'Well, I think you ought to make it up,' I said briskly.

Anna stared at me. The bewildered misery in her eyes filled me with compunction.

'You can say that!' she exclaimed, amazed.

I hurried on, ignoring the implication. 'You'd be wise,' I urged. 'You've known each other all your lives, you've few shocks for each other. You'd rub along splendidly, I'm certain.'

'Yes, we'd rub along,' she said bitterly. 'I'd have been content with that before, because I didn't know what else there was; but now I do, and rubbing along isn't enough any more.'

She was still gazing at me, and there was no longer any escape from the implicit declaration. Suddenly her eyes filled with tears and she began to cry; down her face they poured while she went on speaking.

'I know it's too much to expect that you could feel anything for me. I'm plain and dull and ordinary, and I haven't been anywhere or done anything interesting. I've hardly even met any men, except Tom and now you. I thought that if I didn't marry Tom I'd never get married at all; but now I've met you. I know I'm nothing to you – just someone who's useful.' She rummaged about in the sleeves of her dress and emerged with a handkerchief, into which she blew her nose loudly.

'Nonsense, Anna,' I said firmly, grasping her by the arms and giving her a good shake. If there was one thing I deplored in others it was loss of control, and Anna's had quite gone, and with it her sense of proportion. 'I'm fond of you, of course I am; but you must realize that there could never be more between us.' I was appalled at the idea.

'Why not?' she sobbed, all shame dissolved. 'Am I so

repulsive?' I looked in distaste at the top of her head, now wavering too close to my shoulder. A weeping woman was seldom a pleasing sight. Anna, however, showed no sign of clinging to me, fortunately; I still held her, but she was rigid between my hands and I was made forcibly aware of all her inhibitions. This, more than anything, made me at last compassionate.

'Of course not,' I said more gently. 'But Anna, we've nothing in common. I'm a rolling stone, I hate the chains of domesticity, I have to be on my own. And anyway,' I added, intending to explain, 'I can't marry anyone.'

She looked up then, drawing away from me a little. Her face was red and blotched; desirability was her last asset now.

'Why not?' she asked, sniffing. 'You could leave the domesticity to me. You wouldn't need to think about me much, I wouldn't expect a lot, just to look after you.'

She was pathetic. The conversation had become to me a nightmare from which I must extract myself with speed; and a nightmare was what it would become in Anna's recollection when she had time to reflect. So that she should not feel too much humiliation, I did not, after all, speak about Fenella. I dropped her arms and turned away.

'I can't marry you, or anyone else,' I said harshly. 'For many reasons,' I paused, and then added, 'I'll be dead in six months' time.'

That silenced her. The tears ceased and she caught her breath, red-eyed and haggard.

I pressed my advantage.

'I've just spent a week in hospital,' I said. 'I get ill and have to go in for treatment. One day they won't let me out again.'

'Oh, Neil!' She believed me at once, although she said aloud: 'No, I can't believe it.'

'It's true.' Suddenly the relief of breaking silence overcame my reluctance to enlarge, and I told her all that had happened. She listened quietly, watching me, her handkerchief clutched in her hands and the basket now forgotten on the grass.

'But you shouldn't be alone,' she said at last. 'Supposing you got ill and needed help?'

'The brandy keeps me going,' I said. 'I won't suddenly collapse, I just feel bad. You're not to tell anyone, Anna. I forbid you, do you hear?' I told her sternly.

She replied obediently: 'No, Neil,' and then in a whisper: 'Can't anything be done?'

'Only a few reviving acts, like I've just had,' I said. 'That's all. One day I won't revive.'

She dropped her hands. For a moment she hesitated, and then with unexpected dignity she spoke.

'I'll go now, Neil. First I'll fetch what work you've done since you got back. I'll get it typed tonight and you shall have it back immediately.' She disappeared into the cottage, and I waited there in the garden till she came out again carrying the papers. She crossed towards me and looked at me searchingly. 'Nothing that you've said alters my feelings,' she declared. 'I just wish I could help.' 'Suddenly she reached up and kissed me on the cheek, in a gauche, embarrassed manner, like a child. Now her body, warm and solid, touched me briefly, and then she went.

All life seemed to leave the garden with her: in spite

of the sun I felt cold, isolated and afraid, and filled with an almost overwhelming urge to call her back; at least she offered comfort of a sort. Must I let her go?

It was too late; she had gone, and nothing could help me now, not even brandy.

Anna had left the basket on the grass. I picked it up. It was old and the handle was shaky. In it the raspberries glowed, soft, moist, and warm from the sun; I carried them indoors.

Tonight I would work.

13

Anna

I CAN'T believe it, I won't believe it. He invented it to shut me up. He's been seeing some woman or other in London and he's not dying, he's just weak and unprincipled and he drinks.

All the way home, after our conversation, I felt stunned and incredulous. I just couldn't take in what Neil had said, and it was a shock when Lalage came trotting up behind me on the Fanshawe's grey pony and called me. I'd forgotten all about her.

'Hallo, Aunt Anna, I've had a lovely ride,' she cried. Her face was pink and shining, and her hair, in two stubby plaits, stuck out under her velvet cap in ramrod spikes. She was not wearing her glasses and her eyes had a vague, dreamy expression in them because she could not see distinctly; she exuded joy. 'I've just been walking Joey a bit, to cool him off,' she explained. 'Pam's gone on. Now I must take him back to his field. Would you like to come too?' She peered kindly down at me from her elevated position.

I put my hand to my face: it still felt hot, and I wondered how many traces of the ravages of my outburst at the cottage still were left.

'Oh, no, I won't, if you don't mind, Lal; I've got rather a lot to do,' I said, excusing myself, but I felt contemptible; a month ago, of course, I would have gone with her, and now I waited for her face to fall. But her expression did not change.

'Righto. I'll be quick, and then I can help,' she said, and turned the pony round. Forgetting his need to cool down she trotted away up the road, and I hurried on home, slipping in quietly by the back door so that I could not be seen before I'd had a chance to sponge my face and sort out some of the turmoil in my mind.

It's funny how quickly you can alter: six weeks ago I was just a dull, good girl, doing nothing exciting, only waiting to marry Tom so that I could continue to be good and dull but with the extra dignity of the married state. I used never to think very much about anything, except the next job to be done, like mulching the sweet peas, or trying not to annoy Mother, or the Red Cross collection, or my turn to do the church flowers. Nothing very startling ever happened. We had an occasional crime wave when the village boys came after our apples or got overexcited on Guy Fawkes day; and sometimes there was a little gossip to chew if anyone got married or died, or left the village. Occasionally I went to stay with Marjorie, but nearly always just to help her in a crisis, and though I sometimes daydreamed about meeting a fascinating man in Gerrards Cross, in fact it never happened and the only men I saw were the tradesmen or the dull, prosperous, bored and boring fathers of Lalage's and the twins' friends. No one eligible ever crossed Marjorie's threshold, and soon I stopped imagining that such people even existed, let alone that one might come to Westington.

Lalage soon returned from dealing with the pony. She was hot and sticky, and her Aertex shirt clung damply to her. Mother frowned disapprovingly when she came in to supper still dressed in her riding things, but she had washed, and combed the top part of her hair that was not clamped into the plaits, and had put her spectacles on again. It was only cold beef and salad, with baked potatoes, for supper; but there were the last strawberries from the garden, and a big jug of cream, and Lalage had three helpings of fruit. Mother cross-examined her about school, and the doings of the twins, and tried to be nice, but she doesn't like Lal. I wonder why? Perhaps it's because she can't feel any pride in her, since she's not much to look at and undistinguished in every other way, but I should have thought you'd automatically like your grandchildren. Of course, I'm not as mad about the twins as everyone else is; I think they're spoilt and conceited, though they are rather striking in appearance of course, so very much alike. It's a good job one's a boy and one a girl or you'd never know which was which. Piers seems happy at his prep. school. I thought Lal and Pandora might get on better left together, but that doesn't seem to be happening. Perhaps it's too late; Pandora is already doing much better at school than Lalage did at the same

age, and that's no help. I think it's a pity they haven't
sent Lal off to boarding-school, she might blossom on her
own where she can't be compared, and Marjorie's always
moaning about how hopeless she is, you'd think they'd
wash their hands of her. Still, I know it's hideously ex-
pensive so I suppose they really can't afford it. In any
case I think boarding-school is an awful invention; fancy
parting with your children for three-quarters of the year,
it must be agony. Betty Fanshawe hates it when hers
go back, I know, though she gets a bit exhausted in the
holidays when they're all at home and she spends her
time dashing from the kitchen to gymkhanas and driving
them round to parties. Here, of course, there isn't much
choice in the way of day schools, so I suppose Tom and
I will have to send ours away too . . .

Good gracious, for a moment I'd forgotten. That's not
going to happen now.

During supper, the conversation of course turned once
again in the wrong direction. Lalage wanted to know
when the wedding would be.

'Nothing can be decided yet,' I said shortly. I could
not blame the child for wanting to head Mother away
from talk of the twins and of her own scholastic career.
'Not for ages,' I added. 'Have some more cream?'

'Thanks.' Lalage took the jug. 'Where'll it be? Here?
Done by Mr Gowberry?' she demanded, flooding her
strawberries in a sea of cream.

I said nothing, but Mother answered her.

'Of course it will be here, Lalage dear,' she said. 'Don't
make your strawberries into a pudding, it's so messy.'

'They taste nicer mashed,' said Lalage, undaunted,

continuing to flatten them with her fork. Mother frowned, but now it was my turn to welcome a diversion.

'I quite agree,' I said, promptly crushing my own.

Mother gave me a look which clearly told me she expected me to know better at my age than to set such a bad example, and immediately I splashed the cream and sent a dollop of it flying off my plate on to the table. I mopped it up meekly with my handkerchief so as to avoid sullying the clean table napkin. Lalage grinned at me across the table and winked.

'But about the wedding,' she persisted, maddeningly. 'Will Pandora be a bridesmaid?'

'I expect so, dear,' said Mother.

Father suddenly spoke. 'Anna will want you as a bridesmaid, I'm sure. You're her god-daughter,' he said. He had been silent for ages, quietly getting on with his meal and watching us all. I'm beginning to find this habit he's developed lately rather unnerving; you think he's reading, or eating, or working, and then you find that he isn't at all, he's observing. I'm forced to realize that much more goes on behind his unobtrusive ways than one thinks.

Lalage was astonished.

'I'm not the sort of person who is a bridesmaid,' she objected. 'Mummy said you'd be sure to have Pandy, she's so pretty, and she's been one twice before.'

I was stung to Lalage's defence, and hoped that Marjorie, smug in Gerrards Cross, could feel the wave of pure hate I sent her by telepathy.

'Of course I'd have you before I'd have Pandora,' I said vehemently. 'You'd be jolly good, and I know you'd pay attention and not drop my flowers or tread on my dress.'

'Would I be chief bridesmaid?' Lalage even stopped shovelling strawberries into her mouth to stare at me in awe.

'Yes. Yes, you would be. That's if I had a white wedding, but I might get married very quietly,' I said wildly, becoming bogged in the tangle of improbabilities. 'Anyway, we can't make any plans.' I tried to achieve composure.

'Well, let's go and see Tom after supper,' suggested Lalage brightly. 'I like him. And I want to see the calves.'

Mother looked relieved at the prospect of getting rid of us both.

'Yes, you go up to Combe, Anna,' she said. 'Your father and I will wash up.'

If it hadn't been so awful I'd have laughed. Here was Mother willing to make a mighty concession so as to be spared the presence in her house of the pair of us, the ugly ones, her problem relatives.

Father intervened.

'Tom won't be at home, as Anna doubtless knows,' he said, shooting me one of his shrewd glances. 'He's going round to the rectory to help get the trestles ready for tomorrow. I've promised to lend a hand too.'

We were reprieved, and I sighed in relief.

'Never mind, Lal,' I said brightly. 'We'll wash up, and then we'll take Toby for a walk and you can tell me all about Miss Toynbee and the riding school.'

So that was what we did. Toby looked surprised at this unexpected attention, for he knows very well that I never choose him as a companion if I can avoid it.

Mother is his customary escort; she uses him as an alibi to dodge the chores. We went over the fields and past the cottage, because it draws me like a magnet. Though it was not dusk by any means, a light burned in the sitting-room and I wondered what Neil was doing; drinking, probably. Lalage prattled on unceasingly about school and about her riding, but I listened with only half an ear. In my mind I was going over the conversation I had had with Neil that afternoon. But it wasn't till much later, when Lalage was in bed asleep with her hair re-plaited and her glasses neatly laid on the table beside her, that I came to any positive conclusion. Then I decided to abandon what few remaining shreds of pride were left to me. If I could talk him into marrying me I could look after him for whatever time was left. At least he wouldn't be alone. I would bear the fact that he did not love me. How could he, anyway? It was too much to expect. But hadn't he assured me that he was fond of me? I'd see that he lacked for nothing it was in my power to give him, and I would have a memory to live on for the rest of my life. If I couldn't persuade him to marry me for the sake of convention I would still go to him on whatever terms he might take me. Neil's opened my mind to things I never knew existed; I don't suppose I ever did much thinking before he came. I want to take care of him and I can't bear to be away from him. I'll get hurt, of course I will, and not only by losing him at last, for already he's made me wretched many times with his mockery and his drinking, but just to be with him is to enter another dimension. I don't care what happens to me; Neil is the only thing that matters, and what use I can be to him.

I sat up till two finishing the manuscript. Luckily my room is at the end of the house and no one can hear the noise of the typewriter. When at last I slept I dreamt that Neil and I were being married at Chawton railway station. Lalage got off a train in time to be a bridesmaid, riding on Joey. In her hand she carried a skull; and it was Tom, reading from a telephone directory, who married us, with the words of the funeral service.

14

Neil

I WORKED throughout the night, and when morning came it was done; the pile of manuscript was finished and Anna could do the rest. I felt purged, delivered. I got up stiffly from the table where I had sat so long, writing, and went upstairs. My head was clear and I felt sharply aware of an increased sensitivity in perception. The colours of the paint in the cottage, the feel of the banister rail, the brush of the hair-cord carpet under my feet, all had a unique identity that had not impinged on my consciousness before. I turned on the bath-water; steaming hot, it poured like a miniature Niagara into the green tub, swirling round and rising fast, its heat misting the mirror and window. I stripped, and wrapped, toga-like, in a towel, I shaved. For the first time for many months my body forgot to remind me of its frailty and I felt strong and omnipotent, so that I thought perhaps after all I would cheat my fate, and I lay soaking in the

bath for some time, relaxed, the water concealing my
emaciation. My mind, apart from a general sense of satisfaction, ceased to operate.

Later I dressed in clean clothes and went down to the
kitchen where I drank three cups of strong, black coffee.
Then I walked out into the garden. It was still early, and
the dew on the grass was wet. Wisps of mist curled about
and veiled the sun, and the trees were unmoved by any
wind. A bird, a thrush I thought it was, banged a snail
against a stone with a loud cracking noise, and when it
had shattered the shell, swiftly devoured the slimy in-
habitant. How savage. Nature red in tooth and claw, and
mankind too, for civilization is only a veneer beneath
which we destroy one another even where we long to
love. I remembered Fenella, and then forgot her again
as I walked down to the stile at the end of the garden.
An old man, employed by Cartwright, came once or twice
a week to cut the grass and weed the garden; I kept
away when I saw him coming, and cursed the noise of
the mower for the hour that it took him to complete the
task. His attentions were enough to ensure tidiness, but
the garden was scarcely productive; no vegetables grew,
there were only a few old rose trees and some self-seeded
flowers. The waste, I knew, worried Anna, and she longed
to cultivate the little plot and see neat rows of peas and
runner-beans springing out of the soil. She was right; it
should be so.

A part of me detached itself from my mind and stood
apart, observing the direction of my thoughts, amused,
incredulous, amazed. I had never spared more than a
moment's consideration for the things of nature before;
bricks and concrete, power and motion, ambition, loss

and gain had occupied my mind till now. My lease of
the cottage still had some time to run; perhaps it was not
too late for me to raise a crop of lettuces. I laughed to
myself at the idea, but it was certainly a constructive one
that Mrs Gowberry would approve, and offered me a new
experience. Memories of mustard and cress, grown on
blotting-paper in a musty schoolroom long ago, came
back to me as an illustration of the quick results that
could be obtained in at least some fields of production. I
might even plant a tree, and so leave behind in Westington something that but for me would never have been
there, another plea for immortality.

There were a few cows with their calves grazing in
the field. I knew now that these were an Aberdeen Angus
cross, raised for beef, for Anna had so informed me; and
that because they were not dairy beasts the young were
left humanely to run with their mothers instead of being
kidnapped into an orphanage stable when only a few
days old. I was no longer nervous of the cattle, and now
often walked to the village by way of the field, although
I had yet to grow fond of them. Suddenly they looked
up, distracted, as they had done that first morning weeks
ago when they had given warning of Anna's approach
with Toby over the field. My mind shied away from our
discussion of the day before. Poor Anna! How much was
I to blame, I asked myself, for the confusion in her mind,
and how much had come about through circumstance? I
could not pursue this line of inquiry now, however, for
the cause of the cattle's disturbance was revealed as a
stout, grey pony came trotting up the hill through their
ranks, with a pigtailed child on its back. When she was
some distance beyond the cows, and they had resumed

their grazing, the rider urged her pony on and began to gallop along parallel with the fence, leaning forward, her pigtails flying out behind and bumping on her back. With my newly acquired extra awareness I rode with her, and although I had never been on a horse's back I seemed to smell the leathery smell of the saddle and the sharp scent of the sweat as it broke out on the neck of the stout animal. The child imagined herself winning a race, I supposed, or galloping over the prairie in the role of an heroic cowboy, or as a gallant knight of old hastening to rescue his lady. Round the field she went, passing me, bent low, oblivious of everything except her present state of bliss, her nose pressed into the pony's flying mane.

When she came round for the second time the pony was visibly flagging, unused, no doubt, to such effort, and by the time they drew near to the stile where I was watching they were ambling along quite slowly, the child upright now, straight in her saddle, and looking remarkably well at home there; even to my untutored eye she was obviously accomplished. Over the pony's ears she saw me, and pulled him up. Then she walked him on towards me, smiling a timid smile. I knew this must be Lalage; Anna had described her perfectly, round-faced, myopic, and be-pigtailed, and had said she thought of little else but horses.

My presence intruded upon her world of joy, and I felt apologetic.

'Good morning,' I said. 'It's a nice day for a ride.' The remark sounded fatuous as I uttered it, but I could not think of a better one. Since reaching adult life I had never, so far as I knew, attempted to communicate with one of her years.

'Yes, I came out before it got hot, but Joey's fairly sweating,' she said with simple accuracy, looking down at the pony's streaked neck. 'He's got rather fat and lazy, I'm afraid.'

'You seemed to be making him get a move on all right,' I suggested.

She laughed. 'He can't really go very fast,' she said deprecatingly. 'He's not built for speed. Still, I think he enjoyed himself, didn't you, Joey, old chap? It'll make up for this afternoon when he's going to be deadly bored, poor boy.'

'Oh? Why is that?' I asked. 'What's in store for him this afternoon?'

'He's giving rides at the fête. Sixpence a time,' said Lalage. 'Actually, it'll be quite fun for me, leading him up and down and taking the money, but jolly dull for him.'

Jolly dull for you too, child, I thought, trudging up and down the rectory garden in the sun, but I did not say so. Mention of the fête orientated me again; in my glow of self-satisfaction I had not thought about it, and wondered now if after all I would have forgotten it without the reminder from the child. No doubt, if I had failed to appear, Anna would have come rushing up to find me.

'Gosh!' Lalage suddenly stared at me piercingly. 'You're Mr Addington,' she stated, indisputably, and added: 'Golly!'

'Why "gosh" and "golly"?' I inquired.

'Well, you're famous,' she said, surprised. 'I've only just realized.' She clearly felt her manner so far had lacked the deference due to the eminent. I was amused.

'Have you heard of me?' I asked her.

She shook her head. 'Actually, no. But Mummy told me and so did Aunt Anna. I expect I'll hear of you when I'm older,' she remarked disarmingly.

'Well, I'm not really famous, only among a discerning few,' I said. 'In fact lots of people don't approve of me at all.'

'You're going to open the fête, anyway, aren't you?' she said, and giggled.

'What's so funny?' I asked.

'I was just wondering whether they'd give you a bunch of flowers,' she said. 'Granny opened it last year and they gave her one. But as you're a man it would look a bit silly, don't you think?'

I did think. So far I had wasted no time in considering what would happen during the afternoon or whether it would prove tolerable or even amusing. I had never attended a village fête; apart from becoming extremely hot if the day grew as oppressive as the one before, I did not know what to expect.

'What about your speech?' Lalage said now. 'Have you got it written out?'

'No,' I said. 'I haven't the slightest idea what I shall say. I shall wait for inspiration when the time comes. What did your grandmother say last year?'

'Goodness, I can't remember,' Lalage said. She screwed up her small snub nose in an effort to do so. 'Something about being glad to see so many old faces around – old familiar faces, I mean – and what a lot of hard work everyone had done and now go and spend your money. That's more or less all. You always have to say that at fêtes.'

'Oh.' I was glad to know. At least no great mental effort would be required.

'Anyway, it's sure to be fine,' Lalage said, gazing at the sky. Already the mist had dissolved and the sun was climbing. 'I love fêtes,' she added.

'Do you? Why?' I felt oddly drawn to this simple, direct child, and wondered at what age a female learnt to become devious and subtle; it occurred to me that Anna had never done so.

'Oh, it's nice to see everyone enjoying themselves, and there's always a bang-on tea, cheap, and you can win things at hoop-la and all that,' Lalage said vaguely.

It sounded a doubtful description of paradise, but simple delights had never appealed to me. Perhaps Lalage could profitably teach me how to appreciate them.

'Well, I'd better go now,' she said. 'Joey's got his breath back, and I've promised to help Aunt Anna with all her millions of jobs.' Lalage looked important. 'There's a good old muddle down at Granny's,' she confided. 'Uncle Richard suddenly arrived in the night with a glamorous blonde.' She giggled again. 'They came at about three o'clock and poor Aunt Anna had to rush about making up beds for them. Actually Uncle Richard had to sleep on the sofa because I was in the little spare room and the blonde had to have the ordinary one all to herself. It seemed a waste.'

No doubt Richard shared her opinion.

'I thought your uncle was abroad?' I said.

'He was. He was in Germany, his regiment's there,' said Lalage. 'But he was coming on leave next week anyway. He just got here early, that's all. The blonde was a surprise. I expect they'll get married. I haven't seen her yet, because she was still asleep when I came out, but Aunt Anna said she's very nice.'

'Good. I'm sure she is,' I said.

'I forgot to ask Aunt Anna what her name is,' Lalage prattled on. 'Golly, perhaps I'll be a bridesmaid to them too!'

'Are you already booked to be one?' I asked, and when she nodded: 'To whom?'

'Doesn't it sound funny, "to whom"? So stuffy,' she said. 'I can't ever get that right in grammar. To Aunt Anna and Tom, of course. She's my god-mother. But goodness knows when it will be. Aunt Anna said she'd have me before Pandora any day – that's my sister.'

Such names, Lalage and Pandora!

'She and Piers are twins,' Lalage continued, and I gasped. 'He's away at boarding-school now. Twins are different from ordinary brothers and sisters,' she added, clearly quoting something she had often heard. I realized suddenly how many times she must have been hurt by comparison with the twins, the prettier sister; even Anna had said that Lalage was the ugly duckling. Her jaunty manner was a defence, a mask to hide her scars and a shield to guard her from more. So must Anna have been as a girl, the plain one sandwiched between her more accomplished sister and her brother. In spite of her efforts to achieve indifference, Lalage would go on through life as Anna must have done, collecting slights until she grew blunted and accepting, complaisant like her aunt; heredity had already marked her out.

I wondered if she knew the Hans Anderson story: but Lalage was unlikely ever to be a swan. I wanted to help her, and so, vicariously, Anna.

'You ride very well,' I said firmly. 'You looked wonderful galloping along.'

She blushed crimson and beamed.

'I say, thanks,' she said, glowing. 'Aunt Anna said you were nice.'

'Did she? I'm glad someone thinks so,' I said, laughing. Lalage was looking at me speculatively.

'Tom is too, don't you think?' she said now. 'You know him, don't you? He's jolly kind, he's always got time to talk to a person.' Lalage had suffered from people who had not, it seemed, and I felt thankful that today my extraordinary mood had saved me from being among them.

'He's my landlord,' I said. 'Yes, he's a very decent chap.' Though true, it was the sort of remark Cartwright might have made himself.

'Maybe I'll be a god-mother when Aunt Anna has some children,' said Lalage on a wondering note. I was unable to feel that this was a laudable ambition, although I respected Lalage's right to hold it. 'Well, I really must go now,' she said, in an adult manner, 'if you'll excuse me.'

I thought suddenly of Anna faced, Cinderella-like, with her usual burden of chores and the demands made on her by everyone, myself not least.

'Yes, off you go,' I said. 'Your aunt will be needing you.'

'Good-bye,' Lalage said. 'See you at the fête.'

She turned the pony and, rested now, it trotted off. Lalage turned in the saddle to wave once before she disappeared. I waved in return and watched her out of sight. As I returned to the cottage my thoughts were travelling in unaccustomed directions. By coming between Tom and Anna, however unwillingly, I looked like depriving Lalage of her chance to shine beside a petted younger sister: cause and effect. As so often before, I wondered where lay the end of personal responsibility.

I had not yet seen Cartwright since my return from London; how much blame for Anna's *volte face* would he lay at my door, and would his release relieve or dismay him? I would have to answer these questions, and curiously I felt no temptation to avoid them. Now that my main task, the book, was done, I must resolve some of the issues with which, reluctantly, I had become involved.

15

Anna

GRAVEL clattering against the glass of my bedroom window woke me up at the moment when, in my dream, Tom's voice was mentioning dust and ashes. It took me some seconds to identify the sound, and I was too surprised to be afraid. I had no idea what I would see when I pushed the sash up fully and stuck my head outside.

Two figures stood on the grass below, holding hands and leaning against each other. One spoke, in a hoarse but very penetrating whisper.

'Anna! My goodness, how you sleep, I thought you'd never wake up. Come and let us in.'

It was my brother Richard, not due for a week.

Surprise gave way to anger, and I hissed: 'What on earth are you doing down there?'

There was a feminine giggle, and Richard urged more loudly: 'Hurry up, do!'

'Be quiet, you'll wake everybody else,' I croaked. 'I'm coming.'

I drew my head back into the room, and practical considerations began crowding my mind as I pulled on my old blue dressing-gown and shoved my feet into my shabby felt slippers. A piece of boiled gammon intended for the next day's lunch and now in the refrigerator rose up in my imagination's eye, and the thought of the drawing-room sofa.

Richard and the girl had moved round to the front door when I opened it, and were standing on the step so interwoven that they might have been one person. I felt suddenly shy, and hopelessly old. The girl, who was blonde and very pretty, detached herself from Richard except for one hand, and smiled at me.

'This is my sister Anna,' said Richard. 'Penelope Brett,' he informed me. He propelled her before him into the hall, and with solemn formality she held out her hand, saying 'How do you do?' like a well-trained child.

I shook it awkwardly, at a disadvantage in my dressing-gown and sleepy stupor. Her hand seemed small and fragile.

'Ricky's told me all about you,' she said timidly.

'How d'you do,' I muttered, not very graciously, tucking a hunk of hair that had fallen over my face back behind my ear. Then I turned to speak to Richard.

'What on earth are you up to, arriving at this hour without a word of warning?' I demanded. 'We didn't expect you for another week.'

'I wangled a few extra days,' Richard said, grinning.

He released Penelope's hand and kissed me matter-of-factly on the cheek; then he seized her again. 'I flew in today, didn't arrive till nine and then I had to find Penny. We couldn't get here any sooner.'

He did not enlarge, and I began to ask why he had not warned us by telephone, but my scoldings died away half-uttered, countered by his grin and the pleading, yet half-defiant expression in Penelope's eyes.

'Oh, well, jolly nice that you're here, anyway,' I said with an effort, pulling myself together. 'Sorry to sound so cross, only you gave me a fright and I was having a nightmare anyway.'

'Nightmares? You, Anna? Come, come!' said Richard, shaking his head. 'Too much cheese for dinner is my diagnosis.'

'Come on, don't stand in the hall all night,' I said. 'Are you hungry?'

'Good old Anna,' said Richard. 'We're both starving. I told you she was a sport, darling, didn't I,' he added to the girl.

She blushed and smiled, and I knew at once that the endearment had not yet become a habit.

'Well, keep quiet, we don't want Mother and Father waking up,' I said sternly. 'And Lalage is here too. It's the church fête tomorrow.'

'Oh, heavens!' Richard exclaimed. 'Chaos, eh?'

'Yes. So you know what to expect.'

They followed me out to the kitchen, and I went on worrying about where they could sleep for what was left of the night. I opened a tin of tomato soup and heated it up for them, and they made themselves great sandwiches with the gammon. Soon they were happily tucking in like the pair of children that they seemed to me to be. At last I decided how to arrange things.

'Richard, I refuse to wake Lalage up tonight. She's in your room. She can move in with me tomorrow, but you'll have to make do with the sofa tonight. Penelope must have the spare room.' Until she married, Marjorie and I had shared a bedroom, and tribulation to both of us the proximity had been.

'Okay,' Richard said. 'I can sleep anywhere. The sofa will be like swansdown after a bivouac.'

'I'll go and fix things while you're eating,' I said. Love seemed to have made Richard into a poet.

'Can't I help?' asked Penelope, rising to her feet. 'I think it's awful of us to wake you up like this.'

'Oh, Anna doesn't mind,' said Richard. 'She's used to coping; she'll manage.'

'Yes, I'll manage,' I said. 'But thanks.'

I hurried upstairs as they began to gaze idiotically into each other's eyes again above their plates, and went to hunt in the airing cupboard for the best sheets. They were right at the bottom of the pile, and I broke a nail dragging them carelessly out. Tears of rage and self-pity made me half-blind as I began to make up a bed in the spare room at the end of the landing. Yes, I was good old Anna who would always cope. How ancient, boring and dull I must seem to that pretty child, she so fresh and fair, and I so plain and battered with my hair all over the place.

Before I had finished she appeared and began to help me tuck in the blankets.

'Do go back to bed, Anna,' she said. 'You must be tired. We should never have come like this, but you see

Rick was longing to get here, and we got engaged tonight.'

I had guessed it, of course. She stood, clutching a pillow to her breast, and gazing at me with an expression of triumph and apprehension, after she had made this announcement.

'I'm awfully glad,' I said. 'How lovely.' I tried to put some feeling into my voice, but the only emotion that I experienced then was one of bitter envy for her youthful warmth and of the simple joy that shone in her smooth face. I knew that I had never felt such uncomplicated happiness.

'It's really a secret, till we've seen my family,' she said. 'But I told Rick we must let you know.'

'Oh!' I was absurdly touched. 'I'm awfully glad,' I said again, feebly.

'You'll help me, won't you?' she begged. 'I'm awfully ignorant and silly, but I do mean to be a good wife to Ricky. He's wonderful, isn't he?'

I took the pillow away from her and began to shake it into its case. I wasn't sure that I agreed with this opinion of my brother; in my experience he was selfish and vain, but he possessed unlimited supplies of undeniable charm.

'You mustn't spoil him,' I said. 'Be firm.' I gave her a bracing sort of a hug, and added optimistically: 'He'll be a very good husband, I'm sure.'

'Oh, I know,' she said.

I determined that if ever I saw evidence of anything else I would flay Richard alive, rather than watch, detachedly, while he crushed this vulnerable, vital young creature into dowdy suppression.

'You must go to bed,' I said. 'We'll have lots of time to talk tomorrow.' I crossed my fingers, for it was most unlikely that we would, though I must try to find some. 'There are masses of old snapshots of Richard when he was a little boy that I'm sure you'd love to see.'

'Oh, I would,' she said. 'Thank you, Anna.' She giggled suddenly; it was most attractive, this swift, frequent manifestation of her happiness. 'I'm much too excited to sleep a single wink,' she added.

'Well, try, anyway,' I told her. 'Don't hurry to get up in the morning, it'll be bedlam here as we've got such a lot to get ready for the fête.'

'I'll help you, if you'll let me,' Penelope said.

'I'd be jolly grateful,' I said warmly. 'The more the merrier. Now, pop down and say good night to Richard. I'm just going to collect some blankets for him and then I'll follow you.'

Burdened with my load, I took care to bang against the drawing-room door before I went inside, and when I did enter, Penelope was ten feet away from Richard. She was starry-eyed and tranced, and seemed to leave the room by a process of levitation rather than by the normal method of locomotion.

'Here,' I said briskly, throwing the blankets down on the sofa. 'Thanks,' said Richard, and then, with a more sheepish expression on his face than I had ever seen there before: 'Has Penny told you?'

'She has.' I looked at him. 'You're very lucky, Richard,' I said. 'She's sweet.'

'Don't I know it?' He whistled through his teeth as he began arranging the blankets on his prospective bed.

'Father's a general, too. Nice to have one in the family, eh?'

I stared at his unheeding back and suddenly I exploded.

'Richard, if you ever hurt that child I'll have something to say about it,' I told him furiously. All masculine insensitivity and callousness seemed at once to be concentrated in the figure of my brother.

'Here, what on earth's the matter, old girl?' exclaimed Richard, turning round and taking me by the arm. 'Cool down. Of course I'd die sooner than hurt a hair of her head. What has got into you?'

I took a deep breath. The inquiry was justified. What was it that had suddenly opened my eyes to the prospect in front of Richard and Penelope? I knew that it was the new vision Neil had taught me; from him I had learned a cynicism which made it impossible for me to accept the probability of simple felicity.

'She's such a dear, and so very young, Richard,' I said. 'I'm sorry, I'm afraid I'm rather tired. Good night.'

Abruptly I left him and went upstairs, feeling like weeping for both of them, for their youthful trust, and for the unknown future with its trials and the frustrated hopes which must surely face them. As dawn broke I came to the conclusion that Penelope might chip Richard's centre of self-interest sufficiently to win them happiness. At half past six I abandoned the search for sleep and got up. I felt heavy and dull, and my head ached. Down in the kitchen I made myself some tea and swallowed some aspirins, hoping the combination would do something to make me able to endure the day.

Lalage came creeping into the kitchen as I poured

myself out a second cup; she wore her jodhpurs, and was breathing heavily, creating an atmosphere of mystery.

'I'm going for a ride,' she said. 'Pam said I could if I woke up, Joey's so fat he needs masses of work. I'll be back in time for breakfast.'

'Can you manage all right?' I asked. 'Will Joey let you catch him?'

A wounded look reproved me.

'Sorry, I forgot,' I mumbled. 'Have a cup of tea before you go?'

Lalage accepted this offer, and sat on the edge of the table swinging her legs while she drank it, with the steam from it misting her glasses. I cut her a thick slice of fruit cake to keep body and soul fortified until breakfast.

'Do you always get up as early as this?' she inquired through the crumbs.

'No,' I shook my head. 'I hope I didn't wake you?'

'Oh, you didn't, I was just too excited to sleep,' Lalage said. 'I love coming here, Aunt Anna. I do wish we lived in the country.'

'Well, you almost do,' I pointed out. 'Gerrards Cross isn't really towny.'

'It isn't really country, either,' Lalage said, with truth. 'Not like here. Will you let me come and stay at Combe after you're married? It won't be the same here after you've left.'

I was painfully grateful for this tribute.

'Of course you can come and stay wherever I am,' I parried, and to divert her: 'Uncle Richard arrived during the night. He's asleep on the drawing-room sofa, so we must keep quiet. We don't want him to wake up yet, he didn't go to bed till four o'clock.'

'Gosh,' said Lalage. 'How late. I never heard him arrive. I haven't seen him for simply ages. How did he get here?'

'He flew over yesterday, and then borrowed someone's car, it's outside. Luckily he didn't come roaring down the lane at eighty miles an hour waking the whole village. He threw gravel at my window – cracked a pane of glass, too, I see this morning.'

'Golly, Grandfather won't half be cross,' said Lalage gleefully. 'How dramatic!'

'It didn't seem very dramatic to me in the night, I can tell you,' I said. 'I was pretty annoyed at being woken up.'

'But pleased when you found it was Uncle Richard?' Lalage asked anxiously.

'Oh, yes, when I'd stopped being cross,' I agreed.

'Did you and Uncle Richard fight when you were young?' Lalage wanted to know.

'Mm, yes. We still do, sometimes,' I said. 'Though not with fists any longer.'

'I fight with the twins,' Lalage said. 'I try not to. It's easier now, they're boring, so I leave them alone. They don't ever fight with each other.'

'Twins hardly ever do,' I said and sighed. Poor Lalage. It had often seemed harder to me to tolerate Marjorie or Richard than strangers from outside the family. Manners seldom came to the rescue where there was the bond of blood.

'Uncle Richard's brought a girl friend with him,' I said aloud. 'She's in the spare room. Her name's Penelope and she's sweet, very pretty, a blonde.'

'Oh, goody, more weddings,' said Lalage, chortling.

I laughed. 'Don't jump to conclusions,' I warned.

'It's time he settled down, I'd say,' Lalage said bene-
volently. 'If she's so nice we must hope for the best. No
harm in that, is there?'

'None,' I agreed, getting up. 'Now if you want that
ride you'd better buzz off, Miss Matchmaker. Take the
old bike down to the field, you might as well save your
legs and it'll be quicker. I won't fuss if you're a few minutes late for breakfast, but there's an awful lot to do today, and I'll have to see about extra food now, so don't
be too long.'

'I won't,' Lalage said. 'And I'll help. I'll wash up and
peel potatoes.'

'Good girl, I know you will,' I said, and kissed her. She
hugged me briefly; she felt hard and muscular and solid;
then she departed, her pigtails, irregularly plaited, standing out like paintbrushes under her velvet cap. I watched
her go: if I had married straight from school I could have
had a daughter her age now; and other, younger children.
But I hadn't done that. Tom had been away, still in the
navy.

Why did I think of Tom like that?

Suddenly something seemed to clear my brain; I no
longer felt burdened with depression, and my headache
began to lift. Heartbreak for Penelope did not now seem
inevitable; I thought again of her vivid, joyful face, and
the way she had looked at Richard, and all at once I
knew that whatever I had imagined, this was not the
same thing at all as the bitter, uncomfortable emotion,
all-pervading, that Neil had made me feel. Penelope
understood her own experience, and I did not, except
that I knew Neil only felt for me the same 'good old

Anna' sentiment that everyone else did. He had, at least, never pretended.

My resolutions of the night before vanished as if they had never been made: horror at his plight remained, and I was bound by duty to hold out any help I could towards him, he should not be alone; but strangely, without understanding why, I was freed.

16

Neil

M Y mood of extra awareness persisted after the child and her pony had gone. I was able to stand aside from myself and marvel because it had occurred to me to wonder if my presence in Westington had proved only beneficial to the village. At first, after my arrival, I had considered Anna's life to be one of such dreary negation that my advent must have been like that of a saviour, jolting her mind into channels it had never ventured down before and shaking her out of her dull complacence. Now I was less certain if this was good: would she settle again, after I had gone? Before, I would have thought her weak to try; now above all I desired her return to the uneventful existence she had known and for which nature had designed her. Somehow I must anticipate and prevent the sacrifice of herself which I feared she would offer at the first opportunity. Poor Anna, ill-equipped to deal with a situation she could not wholly grasp. A year ago I would have been unable to resist exploiting her, whether for experiment or because she would demand it; but now I was too tired and too ill, and so she would escape with her life just chipped by meeting mine, not shattered. For some reason which I could not understand I felt obliged to do what I could to lead her back to her former path.

In order to forestall any attempt on Anna's part to catch me alone in the cottage, I decided to take the finished manuscript down to her. She would be so busy with the Cinderella-like chores of her daily life and the presence of so many people in the house that she would be protected from her own folly. It was still very early, so I made some more coffee, smoked a cigarette, and wrote a letter to my publishers. Then, with the manuscript in its folder under my arm, I strolled down the hill and through the village to the Grange. Now each yard of the way was familiar; roses bloomed in every cottage garden, and other flowers, tall and bright, blue and pink, yellow or white, nodded above the fences; I wished I knew their names. The surface of the road was blackened where the tar, under the hot sun of the past weeks, had melted through the chippings. I passed Mrs Potter's shop, closed still because it was so early. Her window was filled with its usual display of sweets and soap, tins and bottles, toothpaste and laxatives, the wares of civilization; a tabby cat, curled in a ball, slept calmly among them. I walked on, past the telephone box on the bend, and the pond where I had first met the vicar; and so at last to the Grange, screened from the curious by its high old ivy-covered wall. I walked through the gateway and up the short gravel sweep to the house.

A red sports car was drawn up outside the front door and a young man with fair hair was industriously polishing the windscreen. He straightened as I approached and looked at me inquiringly, in some surprise. I did not know whether this was caused by my appearance, which was today above reproach sartorially though I knew I looked yellow and haggard, or because of the hour: probably both. He was, of course, Anna's brother, though they seemed to have little resemblance to one another.

'Captain Harris? Good morning,' I began, getting in first. 'Is your sister at home?'

'She's here, but she's very busy. It's early,' he replied in tones of rebuke.

'I know, but I wanted to catch her before she had to go off with her cakes and lettuces,' I said, making an effort to be pleasant. 'My name is Addington.'

The expression of distaste which had appeared upon his features at my advent now deepened, and I realized that he shared his mother's view of me; so does a reputation grow.

'How do you do?' he said disapprovingly. 'Anna is washing up breakfast. I'll get her.'

He went into the house, abandoning me on the gravel, and I amused myself by admiring the car while he was gone. It bore a great many badges on a chrome bar under the radiator; and in the back there was a blue silk scarf, belonging no doubt to the blonde.

Anna came immediately. She wore a red and white checked apron and was still carrying a cup in one hand and a tea-towel in the other. She looked pale and exhausted, and for the first time I felt a pang of genuine compassion for her.

'Neil! What's the matter? Are you all right?' she asked, gazing at me anxiously. 'It's very early.'

'I know, I'm sorry to come when you're busy but I wanted to save you a journey,' I said. 'It's finished.' I showed her the manuscript, and her face lightened.

'How wonderful! You must have worked all night,' she said.

'I did,' I admitted. 'I finished at six o'clock.'

'Oh Neil, then you've had no sleep!' Her manner became at once maternal and solicitous.

'I don't feel at all tired,' I told her truthfully. 'I'm pleased and thankful.'

She scrutinized me. Though so weary, she looked different, less intense.

'You don't look any more tired than usual,' she allowed. 'Would you like to come in, Neil? You'd better have a rest. There's chaos inside but I can find you some coffee if you don't mind having it in the kitchen.'

'Thank you, I'd like that,' I said. My legs ached a little, not surprisingly after their unusual exertion, since I had spent almost a week in bed, and I was glad to accept.

Anna led the way into the house.

'Lalage said she'd met you this morning,' she said. 'So I knew you were up early. She's busy helping me.'

Sure enough Lalage, still in her riding clothes, was occupied at the sink. Steam engulfed her sturdy arms, and she turned to beam at me through her spectacles.

'Hallo, Mr Addington, 'scuse me not shaking hands,' she greeted me cheerfully. 'Afraid I can't see you very well as my specs are all misty, the water's so hot. Hope I'm getting the things clean, Aunt Anna.'

'So do I,' said Anna, manipulating jugs. 'Here, Neil. I've put sugar in. I'd just made a fresh brew for myself.' She handed me a cup of coffee, and I saw that her own was already standing on the window sill. Now she resumed her interrupted task of drying the dishes. 'I'll just finish this, if you don't mind, and then I'll take the manuscript and fetch you what I finished last night. I'll get it done as soon as I can.' To my surprise, she seemed in complete control.

'Don't worry. It's all done now, that's the main thing,' I told her. 'I hear you had a disturbed night.'

'Yes, Richard suddenly arrived in the small hours, we didn't expect him till next week. He's brought a girlfriend too. That car's her brother's, he borrowed it.'

'H'mm, trusting sort of brother,' I remarked.

'Very,' Anna agreed, polishing a cup and smiling calmly. I saw that this was her proper environment; surrounded by domesticity she was at ease, wise in this sphere, and in the company of an affectionate child. The Anna who had been a constant visitor at the cottage struggling courageously with my ill-humour and worse behaviour was not the real woman. I wondered if Cartwright, after all, appreciated and recognized the merit, even the beauty, that was in her uncomplaining, competent character.

'You must have a rest, Neil,' she told me firmly. 'You'll never get through the afternoon without some sleep. It'll be very tiring up at the rectory, and it's going to be a scorching day.'

'I feel as fresh as Lalage looks,' I said, grinning. 'Relax, Anna. I haven't been hitting the bottle.'

She frowned, indicating Lalage.

'I know you haven't, do you think I can't tell that by this time?' she said impatiently, putting the last cup down on the table.

Lalage looked round, searching for more employment. 'Is that all?' she asked. 'Thank goodness!' She tipped the plastic bowl up into the sink and sent a cascade of dirty water over her stomach and the floor. 'Gosh, sorry, Aunt Anna, I'll mop it up,' she added contritely, stooping at once to rummage in a cupboard under the sink for a floorcloth.

'Thanks awfully, Lally,' said Anna gratefully when order was restored. 'You were a terrific help. Now you hop off and get into some cooler clothes and then we'll do the beds.'

'Do you think Penelope's awake yet?' Lalage asked. 'I'm dying to see her. That's the blonde I told you about,' she added to me.

'She'll appear when she wakes,' Anna said. 'Let's leave her, poor thing, she was very tired.'

I wondered how often Anna ever had a chance to sleep late. Life with Cartwright, I realized, would certainly be much less demanding than her present existence. Here she served without any reward of fulfilment; with children, with a husband, though her life would still be one of service there was at least a possibility that she would receive as well as give.

As Lalage left the kitchen through one door, Colonel Harris entered by another, from the garden. He stamped his feet outside, shaking earth off them, and then came in, ducking his head under the low lintel.

'Ah, Anna, Joe's got your lettuces cut,' he began, not noticing me. 'He's putting everything in the car, save you bothering.'

So someone did take thought for Anna.

'Thanks, Daddy,' she said, sounding surprised. 'I'd have done it, I always do.'

'I know, my dear, but you've got quite enough to manage with your brother and that girl on your hands. Too bad of him, turning up like that without a message; he might have telephoned.'

'Oh, it's all right,' Anna said again. I could hear the astonishment in her voice, and knew that she was, after all, quite unused to having concern expressed about herself.

'Thought you looked dog-tired at breakfast,' grunted her father, bending over the sink and peering out of the window, his back displayed to Anna and me. 'Trouble is, we all take you for granted.'

Anna looked startled. Of course he was right, and of course, too, this would always be her role in life. She would be taken for granted as prioress in charge of all local organizations and good-works committees before she was much older, married or single. Even Cartwright might in time merely accept her.

Belatedly, the Colonel realized that there was an intruder witnessing this dialogue, and he frowned at me, whilst curtly saying, 'Good morning.'

Before he could attack me, I disarmed him by remarking: 'I'm another offender, I'm afraid, bringing Anna more work to do, but this is the end of it, and I don't know where I'd have been without her help.'

'Oh well, I daresay she's enjoyed it,' he allowed, grudgingly. 'It was a change, anyway, gave her something different to think about, eh, Anna?'

'Oh, yes,' she said, by now looking thoroughly bewildered.

'Still, I'm glad to hear it's over,' he added. 'Anna's got enough to do.'

'I think she has,' I agreed.

'Give it to me, Neil, and I'll put it away,' she said, holding her hand out for the manuscript. I gave it to her, and she said, 'I'll put it away and fetch the other bit,' hurrying out of the room.

Her father was now pottering about the kitchen looking into jugs in a hopeless way.

'I suppose Anna hasn't got any tea on the go?' he asked me wistfully.

'I don't think so, but the coffee's hot, she just made it,' I said.

'Well, that's better than nothing, I suppose,' he said. 'We had kippers for breakfast, beastly thirsty things that they are, though at least the modern ones come without bones. We don't have them as a rule, but my granddaughter dotes on them, it seems. Have you met her? Lalage?'

'Yes, indeed, a nice child,' I said in an avuncular manner, watching as the Colonel poured himself out a cup of coffee and searched about for the sugar. It was difficult to imagine him as a decisive man of action, though once this was what he must have been; but though he had withdrawn and become a thriller-reading, cabbage-growing automaton I felt that integrity and some insight were still present.

'Yes, yes, she is,' he agreed absently. 'Like her aunt, like Anna. I'll be glad when she and Tom are married. Time she settled down and raised a family of her own. Doesn't do to put these things off too long, especially at her age.' He swallowed a large mouthful of coffee and shot me a piercing look over the rim of the cup. 'Tom's a sound fellow,' he said. 'They'll be well content.' It was a statement.

'I'm sure they will,' I said politely, wondering what was expected of me.

'It would be a very great pity if anything went wrong and prevented it,' he said.

I returned his gaze steadily.

'I entirely agree,' I said, and added innocently: 'Why should it?'

'Why indeed? I'm glad we agree,' he replied, setting his cup down firmly on the table, and as Anna returned at that moment he got up and went back into the garden.

She led me out by the same route.

'We won't run into Mother this way,' she said.

'Would it matter if we did?' I could not resist trying to prick her, but relented enough to add: 'I know she disapproves of me, perhaps it is too early to give her such a shock.'

'It isn't that,' Anna protested.

'Yes it is,' I replied firmly. 'Now back you go to your chores, Anna. I'll see you this afternoon.'

'I wanted to talk to you – I've been thinking—' she began, but not wildly.

'None of it matters,' I said. 'You've got to forget it. All of it. Now go, my dear.'

'There isn't time now,' she said, half to herself. 'I suppose there will be.' And then to me, 'You will rest?'

'If it will make you happy,' I said.

With that she had to be content, and as I left her my determination to take no further advantage of her concern for me was strengthened by what I had observed during the brief period when I had been seated in the kitchen.

My next calling point was to be Combe Farm, but it was too early to go there so I strolled slowly back through the village to the church where, so surprisingly, I had spent such a peaceful hour the day before. It was very cool and quiet inside; shafts of sunlight struck through the big east window sending beams of colour through the glass down on to the stone below. The brasses shone, almost like silver; truly the results of that labour were plain for all to see. I wondered if it had been the only real, positive action of my life; there seemed little else to show as justification for my existence. I sat for a time in one of the old pews; my earlier elation had dispersed now and been replaced by another mood of morbid introspection. My books might have made a few men pause to think, for fewer minutes; more they might have entertained or engrossed for an idle hour; but that seemed a slight achievement. Had they illumined even the smallest fragment of the problem that was life? I asked myself, and could not give the answer.

Presently I left the church, for it was time to continue with my plan.

Mrs Cartwright was sitting propped up in bed, looking a little flushed. The nurse said that she had been feverish as the result of a summer chill she had developed, no one knew why. She looked pleased to see me, but it was clear she had not made any progress towards a gain in strength. Nurse left us alone, and from the books that I had brought her when I was last at Combe I selected one, and read to her for an hour. She was sleeping when I left.

Cartwright was in the yard. I could see his burly figure moving about in the gloom of the barn at the end of it, and I walked over to him. The scent of the new hay was sharp and sweet; piled in bales, it was stacked high up under the roof. The dog, Cartwright's shadow, lay in the shade; he saw me before his master and got lazily to his feet, waving his tail slowly from side to side.

Cartwright heard him and turned. His face wore much the same expression of dubious welcome that I had seen on Colonel Harris's military features.

'Good morning,' I said cheerfully.

' 'Morning. So you're back,' he stated.

'Yes. I've just been to see your mother,' I said.

'Thank you, she'll have enjoyed that,' he said. 'How do you think she's looking?'

I shrugged. 'Much the same. A bad colour,' I said.

'She doesn't seem to improve,' Cartwright said.

'No.'

'How did your business in London go?' he asked politely. 'Everything all right, I hope?'

'Oh yes,' I said. 'It went as I expected.'

He looked at me, and suddenly his wary look vanished and was replaced by an expression of concentration.

'You're a hell of a chap, aren't you, pinching my girl?' he burst out.

I sat down on a handy bale of hay.

'Look, let's get this straight,' I said at once, relieved at having the topic introduced so bluntly, even though I was surprised. 'I never set out to pinch your girl, I don't want to pinch your girl, and so far I haven't pinched your girl.'

He sat down too. 'Well, you've done it, anyway,' he

said. 'You've achieved without effort what I took ten years to do.'

I stared at him. 'Do you mean to say that all that time you—?' Words, for once, failed me.

'On and off. I thought she ought to get about and meet a few other blokes first, but she never seemed to do it. Once or twice I got a bit side-tracked myself, but not for long, and never seriously. Now you come along, and in a month you reduce her to a state beyond description,' he said flatly. 'I suppose she's told you she's chucked me?'

'She said something about it,' I said carefully. 'You want her back?'

'What do you think?'

I knew that I must leave undone nothing that might help to repair the situation. After a moment's thought I decided on the truth.

'I admit that at first I enjoyed teasing her,' I said. 'And I admit that a year ago that might have led to any lengths you care to imagine, simply because that's how I am, or used to be, I never could resist an opportunity. But not now, not this time. For one thing, I've been entirely concerned with my work; and for another, I'm just too damned ill. What's actually happened is that Anna's had a jolt out of her normal monotonous existence simply because I'm a bit different from you and less well-mannered, and she's started to use her brain. One night she had supper with me, and I got a bit high and went as far as to hold her hand. Then I passed right out and she put me to bed, held my head and mopped me up. I've opened her eyes to the horror of alcohol, the vileness of men, and made her very unhappy. That's about all.' There was no need to elaborate.

There was a pause. Then Tom said: 'I suppose you're a swine and I ought to knock your teeth in, if you weren't a sick man.' There was a silence, and then he added heavily: 'I believe you. Poor Anna, it's really my fault. Soon after you came she begged me to marry her at once, but I wouldn't because of my mother.'

'You'll have to choose, won't you?' I remarked.

'There's no question of choice,' he said angrily. 'Anna knew that. It was a matter of duty.'

'I think, if you could have discussed it with your mother, she would have said your duty was to Anna,' I suggested.

'Well, it's too late now, either way,' Tom said. His fists clenched, and for a moment I thought he was going to carry out his first idea and set about me. 'You took advantage of her, of course, you sent her for six, poor kid, you're distinguished, sophisticated – everything I'm not.'

I smiled inwardly at this reluctant tribute.

'She was bored and lonely, that's all,' I said. 'Any man the right age suddenly appearing might have deflected her; but I made her think, and perhaps that was wrong, I don't know. I used to consider it a crime to let the power of thought atrophy.'

'I don't seem to have much time for thinking,' said Tom humbly.

'Well, for some people that may be best,' I said tolerantly. 'But everyone ought to take stock occasionally. Have you ever really put yourself in Anna's position? She's like Cinderella at that place, doing everyone's dirty work and getting mighty little thanks. Most of her contemporaries have a pack of children by now, or else they're career girls, lone units operating quite successfully. Anna's odd man out and very much alone.'

'Thank God she's not a hard-boiled bitch like her sister,' said Tom fervently. I had ceased, all at once, to think of him as Cartwright.

'Women like a bit of romance, you know,' I said, rising. 'It oils the wheels a bit, I've always found. I rather doubt if Anna has any idea of how much you feel for her.'

'I've never mentioned it, really,' Tom admitted, looking sheepish. 'Sounds silly, anyway to chaps like me who haven't got the gift of the gab. It's all right for you.'

'I'd have a go at telling her, all the same, if I was you,' I said. 'Try some brandy first, it helps to loosen the tongue and banish inhibitions.'

'I could do with a drink now,' Tom said, also getting up from the bale of hay. He looked at his watch. 'I've got to take some crates of bottles down to the rectory. Why don't you lend me a hand, and we'll call in at The Grapes for a snifter when we've finished?'

17

Anna

THE fête was due to start at half-past two, and at two o'clock I was tearing down the road to the rectory on my old bicycle, carrying under one arm a bundle of rhubarb belatedly delivered to me at the Grange by Ted Simms, an ancient man who lives in conditions of unbelievable squalor in a tumbledown cottage long ago condemned, but whose demolition has been postponed time and again because of the impossibility of getting old Ted out of it; when the next batch of council houses spring up mushroom-like behind the village pond Ted will be uprooted willy-nilly. I pedalled rapidly, as it was vital to arrive in time to protect my stall from gun-jumpers who would strip it bare of produce before the fête was open if it was left unguarded: before now I had neglected this precaution and spent the afternoon receiving payments from people saying, 'I took a cabbage, dear – I knew you wouldn't mind as I wanted to be sure of it, how much was it, now?'

Lalage had left earlier, not delayed, like me, by clothing problems; she set off, comfortable in her jeans and yellow shirt, intending to brush the unfortunate Joey into a state of glistening glory before he embarked upon his afternoon of promenading up and down the back of the rectory's erstwhile tennis-court beside the rhododendron hedge.

Mother was upstairs, climbing out of her navy linen and into her summer cocktail kit of lavender silk dress and little coat. Father, chafing, was already waiting for her in the drawing-room, immaculate in his grey checked worsted with Old Etonian tie, and occupying the time by finishing *Death on the M.1* which I'd got for him from Chawton Public Library when I went in to meet Lalage's train.

Richard and Penelope had, luckily for the larder, at the last minute rescued the situation by driving over to have lunch with her parents, and they were going to look in at the fête if they got back in time.

I'd put on my new dress after lunch. I'd recklessly

bought it in Chawton, suddenly realizing how dreary my green with the pleats is, and how old, and how shabby my few cottons have got. It's curious, though, how the effect of things can alter in twenty-four hours. I was quite pleased with this dress when I tried it on in *Celeste's*, the only possible shop in Chawton. It must have been something to do with their lighting, I suppose; anyway there's certainly something deceptive about what you see in a fitting-room mirror. This looked nice, quite plain, with pink and white stripes, and a full skirt, which is vital when you've got to be dashing about, you can't start out with artificial string-halt. I was pleased with it and felt that for once I would look reasonable. But somehow it was different when I put it on after lunch. We'd had a frightful scramble, of course, there were masses of last-minute delays and scares; the balloon-blowing pump had got lost and I'd had to rush into Chawton to get another for Betty, who was coping with the Carnival stall but was immobilized as her car has a leaking radiator and is in dock, and Dr Fanshawe of course was out on his rounds in his. We got through lunch all right – the remains of the ham, and I opened a stand-by tin of spam which Lally put away single-handed, and we had cheese and biscuits afterwards as I went on strike over a pud-ding. Lally filled up a few gaping cracks with two bananas and a pear. We didn't take long to get every-thing washed up, but then Mrs Gowberry rang up to say there was no little table to spare for the person at the gate, this year Joe Finch, our gardener, to sit at with the entrance tickets, so I had to fly off up there with our card-table. By the time I got back I'd only got a few minutes in which to wash and change. I put the dress over my head and realized as I did it up that it was another mistake. I suppose I must just be too old for pink and white; it would have been better for Lal and I decided to give it to her, she could easily shorten the skirt. However, I had to stay in it then, there was no time for anything else, so I banged my hair with a brush, wiped some lipstick round my mouth (it clashed, of course, with the pink of my dress), and fled downstairs.

Mother had insisted on having the car for her transportation to the rectory because otherwise she'd wreck her best shoes and also get foot-ache, so as I was late I grabbed the old bike which was leaning against the house where Lally had left it after her morning ride. Luckily she hadn't taken it again. Jumping on, I caught my skirt against the chain, which had long ago lost its guard, and got a great smear of oil across it, so I was well prepared for the rest of the day to be as unfortunate as all these signs and portents indicated.

How I hate bicycles: there was a time when I enjoyed pedalling along without holding the handlebars, swerving about and steering by weight, but not any more. Like my affection for dogs, it's gone to ground. I clanked on down the lane, scattering a parent moorhen and its flock of young in progress to the pond, and skidding on the loose gravel as I turned in at the rectory gate with a flourish, nearly knocking over Joe who was already in position with the rolls of tickets neatly arranged in front of him and a pudding-bowl filling up with money. Over his head a dejected string of bunting, drab and faded, drooped, listless in the hot, airless afternoon.

'Going to be warm, Miss,' said Joe, as I dismounted inelegantly from the still-moving machine; its brakes were poor. 'Shouldn't wonder if we aren't in for a storm.'

I groaned. 'Oh, Joe, surely not?' I protested, sparing a moment to gaze up at the cloudless sky. It was true that a sort of leaden shading, far away, underlined the blue.

'Might keep off till night time,' Joe said hopefully.

'Well, as long as we get plenty of people here first,' I said, 'I suppose we'll get the money.' I went on up the drive and round the house, pushing my bike, and finally abandoned it beside the vicar's dustbins

On the lawn, all was controlled, excitement and anticipation under leash. Ten or twelve trestle tables, the stalls, were arranged in an indeterminate semi-circle round the perimeter, each decked according to the whim of its proprietor and its purpose. Some were festive with streamers of coloured paper or flags twined among the goods; others, like mine, merely wore a white cloth on which were piled in heaps the things for sale. Mrs Gowberry presided over the fancy stall, with various lieutenants ranged around. Mounds of soap, face flannels, tea cosies, Woolworth jewellery, and assorted woollens knitted by the village as it watched television, bedecked her table top. For the twelfth year I marvelled at the unlikely array, and at this strange custom which prevails in English villages: first one is forced to give merchandise to help each stall; then one is compelled to buy back it, or the gifts of others; meanwhile one is also cast as extortioner and saleswoman. It entails hours of boring labour and finally an entire additional day to conduct this commercial enterprise whereby an annual miracle is wrought and a sum of well over a hundred pounds changes hands and is made available for the church. The same result might just as easily be achieved merely by each person handing over the total sum spent in these several ways. It would be far less trouble, I decided, stumping angrily over the grass and into position behind my table, still with the bunch of rhubarb under my arm, and realizing too late that in my hurry I'd forgotten to put on stockings or change my shoes, so that I was still in a pair of teenage brown leather crêpe-soled sandals. A tiny memory pierced my mind: last year I'd found the fête fun, thought it served a social purpose, and had ended it engaged to Tom.

Tom. Consciously, I kept my back half-turned in the direction of the Tombola which he was operating. I was afraid to look at him. In the morning, as I turned in at the rectory gate on my errand with the table, I'd passed his Land-Rover coming out, and had again busily avoided looking at him. I'd not even waved, hoping he would think I needed both hands on the steering-wheel at that moment. I'd just been aware that he was not alone, and when I'd unloaded the table Mrs Gowberry had told me he'd left with Neil. I was astonished, and rather shocked: angry, too, to hear that Neil had been helping him cart bottles up and put them on his stall. When I returned home a little later the Land-Rover was parked outside The Grapes; presumably Tom and Neil were fraternizing inside. I found the thought utterly distasteful.

My stall looked well. It was at least one where the goods were worth their price and would attract custom although most people had well-stocked gardens or bought supplies from us; in any case most of the stuff came from our garden, but as well as the fruit and flowers and vege-tables there was honey, from Mr Ford, a retired bank manager who lived in a new bungalow beyond our orchard and had taken to bee-keeping as a hobby, and jam from the Women's Institute, and eggs. I'd arranged everything, greengrocer fashion, in the morning, for once feeling safe in leaving it all displayed without fearing the threat of rain, for the sun beat down from the clear sky and no wind stirred. Now, however, the atmosphere had changed and I knew that Joe was right; a storm was on the way.

Because of the rush I'd had during the past days I'd foolishly forgotten to provide myself with an assistant. In other years I'd conscripted one of the village girls, always a different one, to help in the first rush. Most of them worked in Chawton in shops or offices, and there were always some with Saturdays at home. This time I'd left it all too late, and so I would have to do without. Lalage would be too busy with the pony rides, and Mother successfully evasive, too much the customer.

I sat down on a chair which I'd removed earlier from the Gowberry's kitchen and placed in readiness. A band of children stood at the business side of the table, eyes level with its top, staring at the wares, and various mothers peered at the jam and bottled fruit with critical inquiry.

'Mrs Bond's, this plum and apple,' one said, picking up a jar and holding it aloft. 'I'd know hers anywhere, real good it is. I'll have this, dear.'

I tried to smile pleasantly.

'Not until after the opening, I'm afraid, Mrs Smith. Half-past two,' I said.

'Oh, can't you keep it for me?' Mrs Smith beseeched.

'There's such a nice cake over there where Mrs Archer is, I'd got my eye on it, and I'll miss it if I wait.'

If I allowed her, then I must also allow all her friends, now pressing round, this privilege; my head was so muddled that I knew I would never remember who'd been promised what; besides, why have an opening time at all if it was to be of no significance?

'Sorry,' I said, implacable.

Suddenly, like the path through the Red Sea, a division broke in the ranks before me, and through it Tom came walking, with a big cardboard box in his arms. It was filled with jars of cream and paper trays of eggs. Over the top of it he looked at me, and I noticed vaguely that he looked tired and hot, before I jumped to my feet, kicking my chair over in my awkward haste.

'Sorry I'm late with these,' he said, seeking vainly for a space on my table where he could deposit his burden.

I scurried about among the lettuces, shifting them so that he might unload. 'I could have fetched them,' I muttered, sounding rude although I meant the words to be apologetic.

Tom took no notice. 'Who's helping you?' he asked, peering about as though expecting an assistant to leap forth from behind the rhubarb.

'No one. I forgot to get anyone. I can cope,' I said.

'I don't doubt it, but it's going to be very hot and you'll get tired,' Tom said drily. He was still holding the box, now down on the table, and leaning across it. He sighed, deeply, let go of it, and came round the table to where I stood. I turned to pick up the chair and struck myself smartly on the shins with it. Tears of pain, guilt and anger came into my eyes as Tom's big sunburnt hand took the chair calmly away from me and set it upright. I would not look at him, but mumbled, 'Thanks.'

He went away without another word, and then I did glance after him. He looked, from the rear, a little shabby in his old grey suit, and somehow he had shrunk. I'd always thought that Tom was tall, but now he seemed to dwindle as he crossed the lawn to where, beneath an oak, his tombola barrel stood beside a table spread with many bottles. As I watched, he took off his jacket, hung it on a handy branch, and began to roll up the sleeves of his white shirt. He did not look at me again, and why indeed should he, I asked myself.

Voices round me brought me back to earth as people asked the price of cream and eggs. I took the things that Tom had brought out of their box, and began to find places for them among the rest. A corner of my awareness, working independently in the bewildered fog that was my brain, knew, in horror, that I had wounded Tom far beyond the depths of any hurt that I had felt myself.

Imperceptibly, the tempo changed: a hush of expectancy came over the gradually increasing number of people on the lawn, and they began to converge slowly upon the small platform where a lonely microphone stood on a single stem, waiting to relay Neil's words through two loudspeakers swinging on the trees and a third hung on the side of the house. Strangely, *The Bluebells of Scotland* came blaring forth, *fortissimo*, and was swiftly muted. I saw Mother and Father walking down the drive having parked the car outside, she magisterial to a degree, and he a pace behind, as in royal circles, and, following that precedent, with his hands clasped behind his back. The music changed to *Rule, Britannia*, and I wondered why I did not know who chose the programme or who worked the turntable. It was half past two.

Would he come?

Visions of Neil flashed before me, and I imagined him lying ill or drunk in the cottage, careless or incapable. But just as I had convinced myself he would never turn up, he did. Dressed in a dark suit, smarter than I had ever seen him, with his hair well brushed and holding himself erect, looking very tall, he appeared from the house, escorted by the vicar. There was a buzz of conversation from the crowd, then a lot of 'shushing'; the loudspeaker gave a scream as the strains of Arne died away, and there was silence. Neil and Mr Gowberry paced slowly to the rostrum and mounted. There was a flutter of clapping. Neil took a pace backwards, folded his hands in front of him, flexed and straightened his knees, and then, with a relaxing of his features that was almost a smile, gazed at a distant tree. The vicar meanwhile strode forward, up to the microphone, peered round at the spectators, dived up his sleeve for a vanishing cuff, cleared his throat and spoke.

A blast of warm air on my neck and a nudge in the ribs, accompanied by the sound of heavy breathing, made me turn round, to find Lalage, panting, beside me, clutching Joey by the bridle. His nose was what had pushed me, and now he sent it exploring among the tempting things laid out on my stall. Lalage checked him and began to giggle. I winked at her, thankful that Neil was all right and apparently composed. Then I put a restraining arm over Joey's neck and leaned on him. He searched hopefully in my skirt for tit-bits, then gave it up and listened meekly to the vicar's speech, only an ear twitching now and then to show he was not asleep

The usual words came from Mr Gowberry, about how splendid it was to see so many people here, how kind the weather, how kind the workers; reference, then, to the worthy cause, that bottomless pit, the church exchequer, and finally our privilege in having here today such a distinguished, although, alas, temporary, member of the community, upon whom he would now call to declare the proceedings open.

He and Neil exchanged a smile and then swopped places, the vicar retreating as Neil stepped forward. I strained my ears so that I would not miss a word. Where I was standing, the sound arrived distorted, part being audible directly from the speaker himself, and part a split second later coming from the loudspeaker relay. Neil looked perfectly at ease; this must be chicken-feed to him, of course. He glanced across in my direction, and for a moment I thought he meant to communicate; then I saw that the near-wink he was sending our way was definitely aimed at Lalage, not at me. Receiving it, she at once began to vibrate again with mirth.

Neil's words were surprisingly conventional, but perhaps it was unreasonable to expect him to find something new to say about a village fête, the pattern of them all is the same. He said that he was glad to be present, proud to be asked, and that he had learned a lot from living, although for so short a time, in a village, which was something he had never done before; that he thought country life contained the valuable ingredient of simplicity which was absent from towns; that the harmonious manner in which all today were working in unison for the common aim was both meritorious and instructive. He did not know, of course, of the subterranean feuds about who should take charge of the teas, or the wounds received over the pricing of gifts for sale, umbrage taken if too low and worse if left unsold. His only reference to his own profession came when he said that an author seldom knew who read his written words, whereas today he was speaking to an audience many of whom he knew personally, particularly, with a glance at Joey, his equine hearer. This sally raised a ragged laugh, and there was applause for his sincerity, which was obvious. I saw then how much Neil had altered: he was far less ready to mock, far more likely to concede that human actions do not always spring from the basest motives.

He ended, and while everyone was clapping I realized that no third person stood on the platform ready to utter the conventional words of thanks. What a frightful black to put up! Of all the things that well could be forgotten, it had to be this that was in fact left out.

Then, through the crowd as it clapped, Tom came boring his way, and as it had divided before to let him pass so now a path was made for him. He struggled into his jacket again as he came, but arrived, smiling and apparently calm, in time to step up in front of the microphone before the clapping ceased. He thanked Neil, and said that while we must be glad, if surprised, that he could learn from our rural ways, he must not forget that much of our lives, ruled by the seasons, was monotonous, and so that we needed and valued the work of Neil and his fellows who stimulated, entertained and even inspired us. I was astonished at Tom; how had he thought of that? He ended by clapping Neil so heartily on the back that I

feared he would knock him down, and they left the platform together. Neil went with Tom over to the tombola,
where such is life, he immediately won his own bottle of
brandy. Having sipped thoroughly by now of the spirit
of brotherly love which seemed to be positively oozing
between them, they conferred busily together with the
result that the brandy at once became the subject of a
spontaneous raffle and ultimately raised five pounds,
eight shillings and sixpence all on its own, being won
worthily enough by Mrs Potter.

The afternoon wore on towards its end. I was kept
frantically busy, for trade was brisk at my stall, where
nothing was useless. Soon my bowl of money was filling
well, and began to hold notes as well as coins. Mr Ford,
given a job in his own sphere, was treasurer, and happily
walked round all afternoon collecting up the pounds before they could get lost and entering all the amounts in a
small notebook. My head began to buzz with the aftermath of my restless night and the effort of being civil as
well as accurate over change. Neil, meanwhile, was
doing all the things a fête-opener should; he made purchases at every stall, managing to find soap and a tooth-
brush at Mrs Gowberry's, and even buying a balloon
from Betty Fanshawe, giving it immediately to a small
child conveniently standing by. I half-dreaded the
moment when he would come to my stall; I was afraid
that he would be laughing at me in my ridiculous dress
and my 'good works' role. In time he came, and I could
discern no hint of mockery as he gravely bought some
eggs and cream. He was by now so laden that I found a
paper carrier bag and put all his purchases into it for
him. He did not appear to be tired, but he had very little

to say, merely remarking that Lalage, down by the rhododendrons, was being kept busy and must have walked several miles at least by this time. Then he wandered off, still attended by Mr Gowberry who had attached himself firmly in the role of outrider. I saw him pause, intercepted by Mrs Timms and made to guess the number of currants in an enormous cake that she carried.

The sun beat down. There was no shade where I stood, and in the heat the lettuces began to wilt and the flowers to die; I hoped they would all be bought before they or I frizzled up completely. The nearest loudspeaker blared 'beat' music into my ears, and my head throbbed.

Some time later, Tom appeared.

'Go and have a rest. Get some tea,' he ordered. 'You'll pass out if you stay in this heat all the afternoon. I'll stay here.'

'But your stall?' I asked.

He nodded towards it. 'Everything's under control,' he said, and I saw that Neil, with his jacket off like Tom, was now in charge, grinning like a schoolboy and busily spinning the drum while he exhorted the passers-by to try their luck. A queue of customers, ever growing, meekly waited for their turns.

I did not argue.

'And get a hat or something. This sun'll give you a headache,' Tom instructed. 'Mrs G. will have one. Don't hurry.'

His voice was cold, commanding and impersonal, and his solicitude much more than I deserved. I could only obey.

Two cups of tea revived me slightly. I sought out Mrs Gowberry, whose supply of goods was slowly shrinking, though a pile of peculiar dishcloths and some ugly china jugs seemed to appeal to no one; with her permission I went into the house and rummaged about till I found a stole less wispy, and smaller, than many she wore. I tied it gypsy-wise over my head. It was orange, but I did not care. I went into the bathroom and splashed some cold water over my face; then I decided to hunt for some aspirins while I was about it, knowing Mrs Gowberry wouldn't mind. I found a bottle of them in a cupboard, and swallowing two, stood at the window for a moment, watching the scene below.

How strange it looked when one was no longer part of it; oddly sedate, and somehow drab. The noise was harsh, but it was mainly caused by the very loud record relay and the curious assortment of music which was being fed to our ears with no thought of a reduced volume. Everyone appeared to be moving silently, for the grass they walked on deadened the sound of footsteps. There were shrieks and cries to be heard, and the clash of wooden balls on skittles as, sweaty and earnest, the village men tensely competed for the pig. I saw Mother queening it below at Betty's stall, holding a balloon and managing to look remarkably elegant, though in fact she despises *chic*. I watched Neil: he looked relaxed and carefree, and I realized incredulously that he was enjoying himself; whether or not it was good for him was, I supposed, by now no longer worth considering. He was talking to a woman in an enormous black hat; she wore a yellow dress, and when she turned round I saw in amazement that it was Nurse Thomson, dressed to kill. I assumed that Mrs Falconer, who went daily to Combe to do the cooking, was looking after Mrs Cartwright. Tom must get a housekeeper, I thought dully; his mother might exist like this, an unhappy wreck, for years, and the responsibility was too much for Nurse and Mrs Falconer alone; he would have to reorganize. Still, it wasn't my business, and no doubt in time he'd realize it himself. I could just see him from the window; he was surrounded by a group of people; the back of his neck, visible as he bent across the table, was burned mahogany by exposure and the sun. I could not bear to look at him, so I hurried on downstairs.

However, I could not let him deputize for me for ever: I returned to my stall.

Tom looked up as I arrived, and nodded approvingly at my weird head-dress.

'Feeling better?' he asked briskly.

'Yes, thanks,' I said meekly, and then with a belated display of gratitude, 'Thanks awfully, Tom. Why don't you have some tea too? Shall I get you some?'

'No, don't bother, I'm just going to commandeer something for Neil as well,' said Tom. 'Quite enjoying himself, isn't he? There's more to village life than he expected.' He looked approvingly across at his protegé. Then he suddenly lowered his voice and said, 'Have you seen old battle-axe Thomson? Dressed to the nines, you'd think she was all set for Buckingham Palace.'

'Yes, I've seen her,' I said, and laughed. Tom laughed too, and for a moment the clock went back so that we were not divided any more. 'This heat's hell,' Tom said. 'Don't get grilled, darling. You'll soon be sold out and then you can escape.'

Down came the invisible barrier.

'I'm all right,' I said, brusquely.

He said no more, but turned away, deflated, and I was left wondering what made me behave so vilely, and feeling bitterly ashamed.

Unexpectedly, relief came soon afterwards with the arrival of Richard and Penelope. She leading and insistent, they came behind my counter and shooed me off again, Penelope declaring that I would soon melt away, which of course must have been obvious, and Richard saying I looked green and might have got sunstroke. I left them to it, gratefully, marvelling that Penelope had managed to get Richard into so unlikely a position after being engaged to him for less than twenty-four hours; I hoped she would long continue to wield such power.

I drifted round the other stalls: Mother I knew would have done what dutiful buying behoved the Grange, but to cheer up two bored girls guarding the buried treasure I stuck a stake in the ground where it might lie, and bought raffle tickets for a box of chocolates and a doll. Then I went to see how Lalage was getting on with the pony rides. It was shady by her track, and I flopped down on the grass where it was cool. She and Pam, both glistening with heat, were plodding gamely up and down, each leading a pony with a child upon its back. They looked exhausted, but grinned triumphantly with the satisfaction of those whose weariness has been earned in a good cause. They had been too conscientious to go in search of refreshment, so I made them tie up Joey and sent them firmly off, while I carried on with the other pony. For the entire afternoon's marching up and down, between them they took the sum of under three pounds, which represented nearly a hundred and twenty journeys, surely the hardest won percentage of the day.

Richard and Penelope had sold out when I got back, and were counting the takings. It was clear that my profits were up on other years. They helped me clear up, and I was grateful but still amazed at this co-operation from my brother.

'We met Tom,' Penelope said, as we folded the sheet I'd used as a tablecloth. 'Rick introduced me. Isn't he nice? And so attractive.'

I was astonishd. I had never thought Tom's appearance one of his better attributes. Penelope was gazing admiringly at him now, as a few last customers tried to win his remaining bottles.

'Oh! Do you think so?' I asked, amazed.

'Oh yes,' she said at once. 'Not my type of course, but for his age and everything, very.'

I looked at Tom too, and tried to see him as if for the first time. I'd known him for so long that I'd never thought much about what he looked like; it had never seemed important, just something as familiar as the local scenery. He's strong, of course, and well built, with an ordinary sort of face, rather weatherbeaten, and brown eyes that look clearly at you. He's got a square sort of chin, a bit jutting; and a wide, firm mouth. He looks nice, I suppose, not ugly or anything like that; but I would never have called him good-looking.

'Knocks spots off that other chap, the writer,' Penelope was rattling on, finishing the sheet-folding neatly.

'Oh, you've seen Neil too?' I said faintly.

'Mm. He was signing autographs when we arrived,' Penelope said. 'Such a queue there was, I was surprised. He's rather odd and highbrow, isn't he? I shouldn't have thought many people here would have heard of him.'

'Well, you see he's been living here.' Feebly I defended Neil. 'I think he's attractive,' I added boldly. I had never discussed masculine charms with anyone before and I felt ridiculous doing so now; it was something I'd never given much thought to, somehow.

'Oh, well, if you like that ruthless, sophisticated type,' said Penelope dismissingly. 'I think he's a bit smooth. I say, why don't you wear your ring?'

I was taken aback. For weeks now I had not worn my engagement ring.

'I'm afraid of spoiling it,' I said quickly. It was true that for this reason I had never worn it while I was working in the house or garden.

'I'll always wear mine, when I've got it,' Penelope declared proudly, and turned to Richard who had just finished checking the money. 'Finished counting?' she asked, and he grinned at her. Richard, of course, even I could see, had everything: charm, confidence and a pleasing face; but time had not yet done much to make or mar what was most young people's ordinary equipment. It was too soon for humour or bitterness, joy or grief, wisdom or folly, to have left their scars behind.

'Twelve pounds, nine shilling and threepence-half-penny here, Anna,' he said, and added: 'What on earth are you staring at? Have I got oil on my chin?'

I floored him by replying with the truth. 'No, I was just wondering what you'll look like when you're Tom's age,' I said. I took the money from him. 'What an odd amount,' I said. 'Thank you, Richard, thank you both.'

'Oh, that's all right,' they said, and walked away, holding hands, and admired by all the village who observed them.

Neil, surrounded by a little mob, was being a success with his autographs. Feeling stiff and self-conscious I walked across to Tom. He was packing up now, a few bottles of salad cream and HP sauce were all that were left. He looked curiously forlorn, alone amid the debris of his stall, which was now in the shade and blissfully cool. I remembered that last year I had helped him, and the sudden, off-hand way in which he had suggested we should permanently join forces. What had made him do it, I wondered, after all those years?

He smiled when he saw me, forgetting how ungracious I had been not long before. Penelope was right, I saw at once. Comfort, and reassurance, came from him, because at heart he was good and kind, and no destructive characteristics had left their marks on his face; the lines on it came from determination, strength and honour, I knew belatedly, and old-fashioned as these virtues might by some be thought. Slowly I took Mrs Gowberry's orange scarf off my head.

'Rather a hideous colour,' I said at random, stuffing it in my pocket.

'I like that dress,' Tom said. 'New, isn't it?' His voice sounded odd, and he wasn't looking at me.

'Yes, I got it yesterday,' I said, astounded. Tom never noticed things like that, much less gave voice to them. 'I thought it was rather a failure,' I went on, desperately. 'Too young. I was going to give it to Lalage.'

'Oh, please don't,' Tom said, turning round. 'You look fresh and lovely in it, Anna. You don't give yourself a chance.'

I stared at him. My headache had come back in full force and the whole scene seemed utterly unreal.

'You're always slaving away for other people, so you never get time to think about yourself like most girls,' I heard Tom go on saying. 'But you always look nice and today you look lovely. And when I read the lessons and you're sitting there in that pink hat you wear, with the flowers on it, it's a wonder I can read the right words, you take my mind completely off what I'm doing,' he went on, bending down over his bottles.

Tom had never talked like this before. I thought it was he, now, who had a touch of the sun, or else that I was dreaming. I watched his hands busily collapsing the table. They were strong hands, large and square, capably carrying out their task with efficient lack of fuss; though he did endless manual tasks and they looked hard and used, they were always, unless he was at work, scrubbed and with clean nails. Neil's hands I could not picture at all.

I began to help Tom. We were silent as we unscrewed the barrel and packed the last bottles in a box he'd got tucked away under a bush nearby. We each knew that we were remembering the year before. Suddenly Tom said: 'Anna, let's begin again.'

I could not reply. There was an enormous lump in my throat. I went on busily packing the wretched bottles. Tom caught my hands and made me turn towards him; his fingers were strong but gentle; it was only later that I realized he was trembling.

'Anna, I do love you,' he said clearly, in a very firm voice.

At last I managed to look at him, and knew, for the first time, that it was true. Once again I had that sudden, wild, unsuitable desire to wind my arms tightly round him and clamp myself against him, but in front of what remained of the fête I could not give in to such an unbecoming impulse. I felt my eyes begin to swim with tears.

'Please marry me, Anna,' he was saying. 'Please marry me next week.'

I opened my mouth to reply, although I did not know what I was going to say, and then the voice of Lalage interrupted.

'I say, you two,' she said without ceremony. 'Sorry to butt in and all that, but do you know where Mr Addington is? There's a lady in a Jaguar outside in the road, asking for him.' She giggled. 'She's awfully smart, miles of earrings and things, and red hair. She says she's Mrs Addington.'

18

Neil

IF anyone had told me, prophetically, that I would attend, let alone enjoy, a village fête, and spend a contented afternoon amid rustic revelry, I should have laughed in his face; in fact, though, the event proved to be a minor revelation.

Astonishingly, I seemed to spend most of the day cast in the unlikely role of Tom's dear old chum. As planned, we delivered his bottles at the rectory, where we found a crisis in progress because the loudspeakers would not work. With the aid of a small screwdriver we remedied this situation, and left the sound arrangements in perfect order; they would be controlled throughout the afternoon by Jim Brown, the postman, who turned his hand, each day, in many directions after he had delivered the letters; he swept chimneys, cleaned windows, did elementary plumbing and some joinery. His annual reign as bandmaster was, it appeared, one he longed for all the year; he presided over a turntable lent by the Fanshawes and a pile of miscellaneous records voluntarily offered by various other folk for the day: the reason he could not mend the faulty connexion himself was that he had not yet arrived back from Chawton where he was giving professional assistance to the local undertaker. As we emerged from the rectory gate, Anna, looking tousled and distraught, drove past us going in; she stared straight ahead and gave no sign of having recognized us, though Tom's Land-Rover must have been familiar to her.

'Some last minute panic, I suppose,' said Tom carelessly.

'Her brother turned up in the night, with girl friend,' I informed him.

Tom whistled through his teeth. 'He wasn't due till next week,' he said. 'How do you know?'

I described my meeting early that morning with Lalage, and did not add that I had already proved her words true during my own visit to the Grange; I was anxious to preserve our new amity by avoiding controversial topics.

'Always was a selfish devil,' commented Tom. 'Nice enough boy, I suppose, in his way, but his mother and Anna have spoilt him between them. Poor old Anna, what a lot of trouble for her. I wonder what the girl's like.'

'A dazzling blonde, so Lalage says,' I replied.

Tom laughed shortly. 'Everything on view and nothing in reserve I expect,' he said with surprising intolerance in one so mild. 'That would appeal to Master Dick.'

'Don't condemn her out of hand,' I protested, though inwardly amused to realize that we were each reacting in the way more normal to the other.

'Hm, well, probably nothing in it anyway,' said Tom, drawing up outside The Grapes with a jerk.

We each sank a pint of bitter in short time: our work at the rectory had been thirst-giving. After a second, Tom insisted on driving me back to the cottage. He pledged himself to collect me again in the afternoon, and said I was to remain concealed inside the rectory until it was time for my official appearance. I was grateful to be spared the walk, and said so, but he drove off with a cheerful wave of the hand while I was still in mid-speech, embarrassed at any display of gratitude. He was, I thought, the embodiment of an inarticulate Englishman. It was not surprising that Anna had failed to recognize his true affection for her. I thought, inconsequentially, of the war, and the undemanding friendships I had known then, soon forgotten, and never met again during the grasping years since.

Bread and cheese, with some of Anna's raspberries that were still left, a little wet and squashy now, made an adequate meal; then I changed, and spent the time until Tom returned checking through the work that Anna had done; she was painstaking, and I knew it would be accurate; there was barely an error to be found, and guiltily I realized that she must have sat up for hours the night before working on it. It would not matter if I had no time to check the last chapter; Anna would transcribe it faithfully.

The mood of the morning was still with me; I felt clear-headed and alert, even cheerful, and began to wonder whether, after all, the doctors could be wrong. In the mirror, my reflection even showed improvement, less yellow, more relaxed; reason told me my recent course of treatment was the cause, and that I was buoyed up with the artificial exhilaration that came from having completed my work. No other weighty tasks lay ahead of me; now I must apply myself solely to the business of living each moment out, fully, as it came, as so many people seemed successfully to do.

Tom came, punctual to the minute. He had undergone a transformation since the morning, when he had been dressed in old corduroy trousers and a faded green shirt; now, he wore a shabby but good grey suit, and a restrainedly spotted tie. His hair was plastered neatly down and his rather florid face shone. He grinned as he leaned across to open the door for me. I climbed up beside him, and with a roar we set off down the hill. I laughed aloud.

'What's the joke?' he asked.

'I was just thinking that it was funny we should be batting for the same side,' I said. 'This morning we looked more like being combatants in a duel.'

Tom chuckled. 'I suppose it is quite amusing,' he said. 'Or would be, if Anna wasn't tangled up in the middle of it.'

'Years from now you'll be glad of all this,' I told him. 'I don't suppose you can believe that now, but one day you'll find it's true, and so will she. You may take a bit of time to sort this all out, but ultimately you'll succeed, and then you'll benefit.'

'Can't see what makes you say that,' Tom said, changing gear at the bottom of the hill.

'Well, for instance, you won't take her for granted, will you?' I could not resist pointing out.

He shook his head, grimly, as we rounded the corner.

'If ever I get her back,' he muttered. 'I wish I had half your confidence.'

'Oh, you will,' I assured him, as genially as the most optimistic Auntie Mabel. 'But she'll be stuffed full of pride and guilt, and you'll have to overcome all that,' I added warningly.

'Well, let's hope you're right,' Tom said as we swept in through the rectory gate. 'I've got to see her now, I suppose. I've been dodging her. I've got a lot of stuff for her stall in the back here. I must say I feel damned ridiculous.'

I saw that he had a large cardboard carton on the floor of the vehicle; it seemed to be full of pots of cream.

'Well, take no notice of that,' I advised. 'Don't be afraid of being foolish.'

' "He either fears his fate too much," ' Tom surprisingly quoted.

'Quite,' I said approvingly.

'I'll mutter it to myself in moments of despair,' he promised, grinning.

We climbed out of the Land-Rover, and Tom, without the formality of ringing the front-door bell, led me into the rectory. Mrs Gowberry, with her stockinged feet resting on a cushion and her shoes neatly waiting on the floor, was spread out upon the sofa reading the *Daily Telegraph*. She rose as we entered, fishing blindly with her toes for her footwear and scattering a little covey of shawls that had been roosting round her neck. She uttered welcoming sounds, and we all began to discuss the weather and wonder if it would stay fine throughout the afternoon.

'I think it will,' Mrs Gowberry declared, hoisting her fichu into place and peering among her curls across to the window. I looked out too, and saw that there was a controlled commotion in progress as more people joined the numbers already gathered on the lawn inspecting the stalls on view. Everyone was apparently wearing their best clothes; there were small girls in stiff nylon dresses, and bigger girls with flowered skirts puffed out above immense petticoats. The general air of prosperity impressed me; there was no poverty in Westington, among the young, though I knew the widows and the retired older folk were not so fortunate.

I was commanded to take Mrs Gowberry's place upon the sofa, and given the paper to read. There I must stay, unobserved, until fetched. Meekly, I prepared to obey, and Tom and the vicar's wife left me. The vicar himself was already at work exhorting on his teams of helpers. I glanced idly at the headlines in the paper: in less than a minute I was sound asleep.

Mr Gowberry woke me, by the expedient of clearing his throat loudly and stamping heavily as he crossed the room. I was astonished to realize how instantly and completely I had become submerged; but now none of the usual aftermath of a midday doze was evident, I still felt clear-headed and alert, and brushed aside the vicar's apologies for having interrupted my siesta. I got to my feet, and glanced in the gilt-framed mirror that hung conveniently above the mantelpiece. I seemed to be tidy, but for good luck passed a hand across my hair to smooth it down.

Mr Gowberry led the way outside and I followed him to the small platform placed ready for our orations at the end of the lawn. Lalage need not have been uneasy, for no one thrust a bouquet unsuitably at me. I winked at her, seeing her standing with the pony in the throng of faces turned towards me. I had thought of nothing to say, but the day was proving altogether so unlike anything I had known before that I knew all would be well, and sure enough, words, adequate ones, came to me. I was brief, in case no one wanted to listen, except Anna, whom I could see draped over the neck of Lalage's pony and gazing at me earnestly. Her mother and father stood in the front of the assembly, she very splendid and intimidating in an unfortunate hat, and frowning disapprovingly throughout my remarks, though they were harmless enough; the colonel stood beside her, looking distinguished and slightly bored, as no doubt he was, but at the end of my address he nodded briskly and began to clap. Suddenly Tom materialized from nowhere, and launched unexpectedly into a speech of thanks; I was surprised that in our new-found concord he had not warned me that this task was his, until it occurred to me, observing one or two faces, that no one had remembered the need for this formal duty until now. My opinion of Tom's vision and resource rose still higher; I hoped Anna had appreciated what had happened.

Mr Gowberry guided me round among the stalls, and I

put into practice what I had already divined was my obligation by buying a curious miscellany of articles. A small girl wearing a dress patchworked all over, front and back, with pockets, ransomed me for sixpence, the price of picking one, and I acquired a pink plastic comb wrapped in yellow tissue. If any of my London cronies, those whom I had once considered were my friends, had seen me, how they would have mocked. But I was content.

It seemed, at last, that my official duties were over, and it was not yet time for my advertised autographing venture. I watched Tom operate his drum, admiring his easy friendliness with all who came along; it was clear that he was popular, and I thought he was a more useful member of the population than I, with my zest for fault-finding and cynicism. During a lull he spoke to me.

'Look at Anna. She's grilling in the sun, that table of her's hasn't a bit of shade. She'll get sunstroke.'

It was true. Whereas every other table had some small degree of shelter from the glaring sun, Anna's had none.

'The lettuces will wilt,' I said.

'So will Anna. She is, look at her,' Tom said angrily. 'She forgot to find a helper, too; usually some child lends her a hand. Do you think you could manage this thing for a bit while I go and make her have a rest?'

'Surely,' I said at once, and eagerly stepped forward to take charge. Mrs Potter from the post office rejoiced my heart by winning a bottle of rich red Tonic Wine, and presently a magnificent lady in an Ascot outfit whom I incredulously identified as Nurse Thomson won a phial of smelling salts.

Tom returned after a long interval; he looked dejected,

but carried a tray with two cups of tea upon it and a large plateful of tomato sandwiches, which we shared. Then it was time for my hour of scrawling signatures in an increasingly flowing style on countless sheets of paper. I found the demand flattering, although I was aware that it came from a spirit of wanting to miss nothing rather than of appreciation for me. Finally, when the customers petered off, I escaped with my carrier bag filled with trophies, and made my way slowly up the hill, across the fields, towards the cottage. I did not hurry, for the bag was heavy, and now at last I felt fatigued. Below, the music from the loudspeakers and the babbling voices faded into a blur of distant sound; and the rectory dwindled till it vanished out of sight behind its screen of trees. I began to feel hot, and faintly dizzy; gone was my earlier elation. At last, a little frightened, I sank down to rest in the shade of one of Tom's tall, bramble hedges, where the cattle in winter would find shelter from the wind. Slowly, strength returned, but I lay there for some time; perhaps I slept; I did not know how long it was before I rose again and stumbled on, angry with myself for not waiting until Tom could take me back. It was cooler now; the sun was low, and it was evening.

Something glinting, silver-bright like a mirror, through the hedge across the garden, caught my eye as I came over the brow of the hill towards the stile. I walked round to the front of the cottage before going in to see what had caused it, and saw that a large green car, a Jaguar, was parked outside, with the sinking sun dazzlingly reflected from its windscreen. I was not really surprised at all to find, when I entered the sitting-room, blinking in the sudden gloom, Fenella waiting.

No one spoke. She rose slowly from the chair where she was seated, and I saw that she still moved with a controlled grace that was almost feline. I had forgotten, or so it seemed, how tall she was.

'You've been a long time getting here,' she said, and with the sound of her voice a host of hidden memories sprang at me.

'I came over the fields,' I said. My heart was thumping uncomfortably, and the dryness in my mouth made me fear that I might feel faint again.

'It's been rather a hot day for a walk,' Fenella said. She was speaking carefully, watching me intently: I wondered if I looked very different; how had she found me, and why?

'Nice car you've got,' I said, reaching for the cigarettes.

She was already smoking. Now she sat again, relaxed, one long, slender hand resting on the arm of the chair, her fingernails brilliant red against the green of her dress.

'Isn't it?' she agreed. 'I've hired it.'

'Well, how about a drink?' I said. I ran my tongue round my mouth; for hours I had not thought of brandy, but now I felt that without some at once I should not survive the next ten minutes. I collected myself together enough to cross the room and find the bottle and two glasses. 'Would you prefer something else?' I asked her, remembering her taste for other things. But she shook her head, and I was glad, for I had not troubled to stock spirits in variety.

'That will do me very well,' she said.

I slopped some soda into both the glasses, and weaved my way over the floor to hand her the weaker mixture.

'Sköl,' she said, regarding me over the rim of the glass.

'Sköl,' I managed to reply, and gulped down half my nearly neat glassful. I began at once to feel better, and sat down.

'So you've been at the village fête,' said Fenella, and I heard the mockery in her tone. 'That's a new departure for you, Neil. How did you manage to get let in for it? Or did it appeal to your vanity?'

'My reputation – any sort – hasn't reached Westington,' I said shortly. 'I enjoyed the afternoon.' Then I could not resist asking, 'How did you know where I'd been?'

'It didn't need much enterprise to read the posters pinned to every tree, advertising the affair, with your name in top billing,' she said derisively. 'Anyway, I've been there too. I could hardly avoid it, since I had to come past, and roistering villagers were swaying homewards clutching their spoils.'

This ought to have made me laugh too; but it did not.

'They had a good time, and it was a worthwhile gathering,' I said, hating the sneer that was being cast upon my new friends and their affairs.

'Come off it, Neil,' she said. 'You've got yourself bewitched by rural charms, I suppose. In six months' time you know you'll wonder how on earth you endured such boredom.'

I did not reply, and suddenly she stopped laughing and stared down at her drink, rubbing one hand against the glass in a gesture that betrayed her inner lack of ease. Her rings flashed and sparkled. There was silence.

'How did you know?' I asked at last, heavily.

She spoke quickly then.

'Vernon told me. He wrote. You're not to be cross, Neil. He was quite right. That's why I'm here.'

But I was furious.

'I should never have told him. He swore he'd never tell,' I fumed. 'It's none of his business; he's my publisher, not my uncle.'

'He was right,' Fenella said again. 'He said you'd buried yourself in some dreary hermitage and were hurrying – hurrying things on by working harder than he'd ever known you do before.' She paused, and then said, with strange humility, 'It's good, Neil. I was reading it while I waited.'

I saw then that she had the typescript of my book beside her. Before I could explode in rage again she went on talking.

'Don't waste time scolding, Neil. You'd left the place unlocked and the manuscript was sitting on the table for anyone to see – or pinch, for that matter.'

I sighed, defeated. It seemed best to try another tack. 'How did you find the cottage?'

'A fat child in jeans, with plaits and glasses, pointed out the way,' Fenella said, lapsing into facetiousness again. 'Once on the hill there was no other dwelling. It seems pleasant enough, I must say,' she allowed, looking round. 'The child seemed to know you.'

'That was Lalage.' Involuntarily I smiled at the thought of her, peering steadfastly from behind her spectacles and no doubt breathing heavily as she directed Fenella.

'God, what a name! One of your dear new pals, I suppose.'

'Yes, and so what?' I said belligerently, getting up to refill my glass.

'Should you do that?' Fenella asked, instead of replying to my challenge. She watched anxiously as I poured myself out another tot.

'Probably not, but what difference does it make?' I said, doing my best to walk very steadily back to my seat. 'Now, what do you want?' I demanded. 'Why have you come?'

She was silent for a time, long enough for me to realize that already we had begun to prick and fret at one another.

'I want to help you, Neil,' she said at last. 'I want to help you bear this awful thing, if it must happen. I don't want you to be alone. I want to be with you.' Her sentences came in little bursts, staccato.

I waited.

Fenella looked a little desperate.

'We can go to France,' she said. 'A villa, near the sea. Some friends of Vernon's will let us have it. You might get better.' It was forlornly said.

'Pray for a miracle,' I said shortly. 'We'd be at each other's throats again in no time. You know we would. Look at us now.'

'It's because I'm scared,' she said at once. 'Oh, Neil, you must agree. You must let me. All these years, since I left you, I've been chasing rainbows; but that's all they ever were. You see, I'm back again. Please let me stay.'

'But, Fenella, we've met again after five years and here we are beginning to quarrel already,' I insisted.

'It's all my fault,' she said again. 'It's because I don't know what to say. I was afraid, when you didn't come, that I was too late already.'

I watched her while she went on speaking. What image of herself had she got obsessed with now? Nature never meant her as a ministering angel. Was it possible that she still had some feeling for me? I knew very well that no other woman had ever been able to displace Fenella from her place in what, for lack of a better description, I could only call my heart.

'That child with the ridiculous name said you'd already gone home,' she was saying. 'I've been waiting here for you for nearly two hours. I was afraid you'd been taken ill, perhaps collapsed somewhere. I didn't know where to look for you, or who to ask. That's why I've been so wretched to you, I've been so frightened.' She began to cry. I had never seen her weep before, although often enough I'd tried to make her and been reduced to impotent anger at my failure. She was never afraid or at a loss. Now I could not bear to see her weakness. Whereas Anna in tears had merely rather sickened me, Fenella stirred me with compassion. I must make her stop this revelation; I must help her to return to her normal state of utter composure. I must, it seemed, at least let her have her way; so, she would not be heavy on my conscience. It might work out; if it did not, I at least had nothing more to lose, and she would have no cause for self-reproach.

So I would not grow my lettuces after all. Perhaps I never would have tried, perhaps the brandy would have tempted me away from them. Perhaps the people of Westington would have forgotten me again and let me brood alone, drinking and remembering. It would be better to go; better to go on a peak, too, before my stock had time to fall, before I viewed my new friends with the eye of disillusion, as I might. Before it was too late.

'France is a good idea, Fenella,' I said aloud.

19

Anna

IT's all over now. I'm back at the beginning; everything is at it was before, and yet nothing will ever be quite the same again. Beneath the surface so much is altered.

The morning after the fête I sent Lalage up to the cottage with the last chapters of Neil's book. Ignorant as I was, I knew that its publication would win him respect and recognition that might make a lasting mark in literature. I'd worked on it for hours during the night, after everyone had gone to bed, wanting to get rid of it, to be finished and done; I'd gone to bed at last, and set my alarm clock for half past five, so that I could, after some rest, resume the work, but I'd been quite unable to sleep. After tossing and turning, trying not to wake Lally, who was now in my room, at length I gave up and took the typewriter downstairs to the kitchen, where no one would hear the noise it made. So I got to the end of it, profoundly moved by the strange, rather mystic story that it told. But after that, I could not take it up to Neil myself.

Lalage was eager to undertake the errand; she set off blithely, immediately after breakfast. She was gone for an hour, and when she returned she was important with her news.

'They're going,' she said, bursting into the kitchen, where as usual I was busy, this time getting lunch under way before we went to church. I could think of no valid excuse for being absent from this weekly habit; indeed, I might as well be miserable at matins as anywhere else.

Half of me longed to hear every item of information that Lalage could impart; half never wanted to hear Neil's name mentioned again. However, she was in any case determined to reveal all she knew.

'They're busy packing,' she continued. 'Gosh, that's a super Jag. She's nice, in a posh sort of way, a bit too dressed-up for my liking. She's called Fenella. Isn't it a nice name? She said it was a bit like mine, the same sort of thing, like Pamela and Daphne. Funny, I'd never thought of names being like each other before.'

'Saints' names are,' I said. 'Go on.'

'Well, she gave me a glass of milk, said they needed it to be finished. Of course, I was quite glad of it. And biscuits.' She paused, thinking hard. 'Oh, he said to thank you very much for doing the old book; he said you'd been wonderful in every way and he thanked you for everything.' Here Lalage visibly cudgelled her brains in an effort not to forget any part of her message. 'Oh, and he wishes you and Tom all the best.'

I went on shelling peas. Lalage came and picked a pod up out of the bowl. She split it, and absently stuffed the raw peas into her mouth. Alternately thereafter she fed herself and the colander.

'I told Mrs Addington how surprised we all were to hear about her,' she said artlessly. 'I said we'd thought Mr Addington wasn't married.' I pictured her sitting in the kitchen, drinking milk, and innocently discovering the answers to all the questions that had buzzed round the village the night before after the Jaguar had so conspicuously arrived and swept up the hill.

'Of course, I didn't like to ask why she wasn't here all the time,' Lalage went on. 'Maybe she had an aged mother she had to look after or something, like Tom. Anyway, they seemed very happy. It was fun. Being married must be quite nice, I should think. Anyway, now they're going to France, to somewhere by the sea, for Mr Addington to get strong. Did you know he'd been very ill, Aunt Anna?'

'Yes, I knew.'

'Well, I expect he'll be all right now, with her to look after him,' Lalage said in a satisfied manner. 'I'm glad; he must have been lonely, all on his own. I suppose he writes books for company. Anyway, he seemed jolly pleased with everything; he kept laughing; they both did. I enjoyed myself.'

'Good, dear,' I said. 'Thank you for going. Now it's time to get tidy for church.'

'I haven't got a hat,' Lalage said hopefully.

'Doesn't matter, you don't need one. Brush your top-knot.'

She departed, reluctantly, and I put the joint into the oven, hoping, as I did every Sunday, that it would survive unwatched and unbasted. Each week, despite my fears, I rescued it before it became a cinder. Then I followed Lalage upstairs to wash my hands and comb my hair, and to put on the pink hat with the flowers round the crown.

There was something I had planned to do: what was it? Then I remembered. Every Sunday since Neil came I had worn my gloves all through the service to hide the fact that I was not wearing my ring, the ring that Tom had given me. Yesterday, before Lalage brought her news, I'd decided to wear it today. I'd put my half-crown ostentatiously into the bag when Tom took the collection, so that he would see, and I hoped he would understand. I didn't feel that I could ever speak to him about what had happened; but if he could let it lie behind us, unmentioned, undisturbed, I would be able to go forward. But now it was different. He'd think Fenella's coming had made me change my mind. While I'd been thinking this, I'd been slowly getting out the navy-blue leather box with the velvet lining where the ring lived. It's a lovely ring, rubies and diamonds; when Tom gave it to me I was speechless because it was so beautiful, and I could hardly thank him. It had belonged to his grandmother, he'd said, and he'd had it reset, specially. He said we could sell it and get something different if I wanted, but of course I thought it was gorgeous. Now I took it out of the box. It was weeks since I'd worn it. While I was looking at it, Lally came in; she'd been gossiping with Penelope all this time; they'd made a hit, those two, and Lally'd got herself all fixed up as a bridesmaid: it's good for her to be liked. 'A friend is someone who likes you,' as it said in that heavenly little book I found at Christmas and gave her among all those pony stories she wanted; she and Tom sat on the sofa reading it after church. It's chaos having Marjorie and everyone for Christmas; I suppose they'll come again this year. Trust Marjorie to push the puddings on to me. If I were married by Christmas someone else would have to cope; Mother and Father might go to Gerrards Cross for a change. I wondered how serious Tom had been about our getting married next week. What if I agreed? But we couldn't, I supposed. It wouldn't be possible.

'Aren't you ready, Lal?' I asked, as she lunged across the room towards me.

'Shan't be a tick,' she said, seizing my comb and dragging it through her hair. Then she saw the ring in my hand. 'That is a super ring old Tom coughed up with,' she said. 'Much nicer than hers.'

'Whose?' I asked.

'Mrs A. She was groaning under rings,' Lalage said. 'Six at least, four on one finger, I counted, and several on each hand,' she added, as if Fenella was an octopus. 'Green things, and masses of huge diamonds.' She poked the comb into the ends of her plaits. 'Buck up and put it on, Aunt Anna.'

I was too weak to disobey; but I put my gloves on.

Lalage then echoed Penelope. 'If I had a ring like that I'd always be flashing it under people's noses,' she observed, marching towards the door. 'Still, I suppose gardening and washing up wouldn't be very good for it.' She disappeared, and I heard her noisily descending the stairs in a series of leaps.

More slowly, I followed. I'd put on the pink-striped dress again. It seemed a pity not to, after Penelope had spent ages getting the oil-stain out for me; it was nice of her to bother. We trooped off to the cars. We never walked to church. Mother wouldn't, and I was never ready in time. Lalage climbed into the minute space at the back of the red sports car, and went off with Richard and Penelope. Father drove Mother and me. He'd been very silent all morning, shooting more of his shrewd looks at everyone, and he'd said very little about the fête or anything else, except to praise the speeches and commend Tom's presence of mind, not that I think Neil would have noticed or minded if he hadn't been thanked, but someone would have. We followed the noisy little sports car down the drive, sedately, and through the village. Father dropped us at the lych gate and went to turn. He parked the car, and we waited for him. As he walked back towards us a long, low car glided slowly down the lane: it was a green Jaguar. For a hysterical moment I thought it was going to stop and that Neil and Fenella were coming to church; but it went on, quite slowly, and passed us. I could see suitcases and coats on the back seat. Fenella wore a vague smile, and Neil waved; I saw that she was very beautiful, and that he looked calm. Then they were gone.

After that, we clattered into church.

It seemed rather an anti-climax when, after all, Tom did not come. Father read the first lesson as usual, and Mr Gowberry read the second. Afterwards, I hurried home as usual, leaving the others having a social get-together on the path and minutely discussing the fête and the princely sum it had, as always, raised; the annual miracle. No one came home for ages; lunch was late. When they did arrive they explained that they had all been round to the Fanshawes for drinks. It was silly of me to feel slighted because I hadn't been there too: it was my own fault for rushing off so quickly when the service ended, and even if Betty had telephoned I should probably have invented some excuse and still not gone. Lally, of course, was out on the pony as soon as she could change from her dress to her jeans.

It was close and oppressive. I sat in the kitchen reading the Sunday papers while the potatoes boiled; outside, the sky was leaden. The storm had held off, but it would not do so for very much longer. I thought I heard a vague, distant rumble of thunder.

After lunch everyone disappeared. Lalage returned to the Fanshawes, for Betty had arranged to take her and Pam swimming. I thought they would get dampened by the heavens before they reached the sea. Father took *The Sunday Times* to the study, where it was cool, and Mother vanished. I knew she had gone upstairs to lie down, although she would never give voice to such an intention. Richard and Penelope went off in the car to see some friends. Even Toby was dozing peacefully on the back step. The wise action for me would be to do the same; for once I had no tasks waiting, and I had arrears of sleep to catch up on, but I felt too restless. I went out into the garden, wandered around aimlessly for a time, and then slowly began to walk up the hill towards the cottage, explaining to myself that I ought to see if it was locked, though Neil had presumably made some plan or other with Tom.

Inside, everything was tidy and clean; for all her exotic appearance, Fenella had not been idle. There was no trace of Neil's tenancy, except the empty bottles in the dustbin and the pile of neatly folded linen in the bathroom; no other sign that he had lived there remained. I went into the sitting-room and crossed over to the sofa; yes, perhaps there was just a suspicion left of the brandy stain from the spill on that first day: what ages ago it seemed. The cottage was just as it had been before he came, and yet in a way it would never be the same again. I wondered if I would ever be able to come here without remembering him; I wondered how much of what I'd felt had been a true emotion, and how much false, imagined, because I loved the cottage and was bored. I wanted to be back where I'd been before, and yet in a way I didn't; I felt that, if I could only find it, something valuable might come from all the stupidity and unhappiness for which I'd been to blame.

I was very tired. I sat down on the sitting-room floor and leaned my aching head against the sofa. I felt sticky with the sultry heat; outside, the sky was nearly black, and the sound of thunder grew steadily louder. I thought that I had been rather silly to come up here; now I should have to wait until the storm passed before I could go. I hated thunder and was rather afraid of it; I certainly wouldn't set boldly out for home while lightning zig-zagged in the sky. I closed my eyes for a while, but even behind the lids I was aware of the brilliant flashes in the sky outside, and the increasing noise. After a time I crossed to the window: trees were swaying, and the livid streaks in the sky made jagged splashes in the navy blue of all the world outside. I sat down on the sofa, shut my eyes again, and put my hands over my ears.

A few minutes later I had a worse shock than the fear of the storm. Someone touched my arm. I jumped up, aghast, blinking as my eyes played tricks after being squeezed so firmly shut, and saw Tom.

'It's only me,' he was saying quickly, knowing he had given me a terrible fright, but I hardly heard him because I was so busy clutching hold of him.

We stayed there, sitting on the sofa, for a long time, while the storm raged, and gradually grew less as the rain teemed down. After a while I hardly noticed the noise. Tom just held me gently, and patted me from time to time while I cried into his handkerchief and all over his jacket, which was wet already from the rain. After quite a long time we began to talk, but we didn't get very much farther than each of us blaming ourselves for all that had gone wrong before he started kissing me. Afterwards, I knew that it was Tom I would always think of if I came to the cottage when it had been sold, and this was the afternoon I would remember.

He'd gone down to the Grange after lunch, and finding no one about except Father asleep in his study, he'd guessed where I'd be.

'I knew they'd gone,' I said at once, quickly, guiltily.

'I know,' Tom said. Then he explained that Neil had been to say good-bye and settle the rent, and had asked him to thank me for the work I'd done. He'd given Tom an enormous cheque, partly in payment for my labours, but partly because he wanted us to buy ourselves a wedding present with it. He'd given it to Tom because he'd thought I'd be proud and tear it up, and so I should have done.

Tom let go of me with one arm and fished about in his pocket till he managed to extract the pink slip. It was for a hundred and fifty pounds: written in Neil's spiky writing and with his neat signature. I gaped.

'He said he owed you forty at least for all your work, Tom said. 'I think we ought to accept it, darling. He wanted us to, poor chap. Let's get a washing-up machine.'

The thought of Neil's money being spent this way was comic: I knew he'd enjoy the joke; and if I thought of him while the water swirled around the crockery, in such a context it would not be wistfully. We'd hear of him again one day, inevitably and with sorrow: that must be faced, and the cruel truth accepted.

'All right,' I said, and as another clap of thunder sounded, shivered and twined myself more closely still into Tom's arms.

'I'm glad we had such a storm,' Tom said ambiguously.

'Why?' I asked.

'Well, it fairly drove you at me, as a refuge, didn't it?' he said.

It wasn't until we were walking down the hill again towards the village that he told me his mother was dead, and that was why he hadn't come to church. She'd had another heart attack, and gone quite quickly, peacefully.

Above us, the sky grew brighter, and the air was fresh after the rain. The grass in the meadow was wet and shining, and all the birds were twittering, bathing themselves and preening their feathers. Down in the hollow lay the village, roofs still gleaming from the water, all the colours sharper now, and bright; and to the east, cream against the green, Combe.